SURGEON IN A WEDDING DRESS

BY
SUE MacKAY

D1476429

MILLS & BOON

All the characters in this book have no existence outside the imagination of the author, and have no relation whatsoever to anyone bearing the same name or names. They are not even distantly inspired by any individual known or unknown to the author, and all the incidents are pure invention.

First published in Great Britain 2011
by Mills & Boon, an imprint of Harlequin (UK) Limited.
Harlequin (UK) Limited, Eton House,
18-24 Paradise Road, Richmond, Surrey TW9 1SR

© Sue MacKay 2011

ISBN: 978 0 263 88618 4

Harlequin (UK) policy is to use papers that are natural, renewable and recyclable products and made from wood grown in sustainable forests. The logging and manufacturing process conform to the legal environmental regulations of the country of origin.

Printed and bound in Spain
by Blackprint CPI, Barcelona

ERDINGTON LIBRARY

With a background working in medical laboratories, and a love of the romance genre, it is no surprise that **Sue MacKay** writes Medical™ Romance stories. An avid reader all her life, she wrote her first story at age eight—about a prince, of course. She lives with her husband in beautiful Marlborough Sounds, at the top of New Zealand's South Island, where she can indulge her passions for the outdoors, the sea and cycling.

Also by Sue MacKay:

RETURN OF THE MAVERICK
PLAYBOY DOCTOR TO DOTING DAD
THEIR MARRIAGE MIRACLE

**These books are also available in ebook format
from www.millsandboon.co.uk**

To Tania
For all the moments we have shared,
and the moments to come.

And
Kate David: the newest and very supportive member
of the Blenheim Writers' Group.

CHAPTER ONE

NEW YEAR'S DAY. Resolutions and new beginnings.

'Huh.' Sarah Livingston scowled. As if anything new, or interesting, was likely to be found down here in the South Island, so far from the cities. Thanks to her fiancé—very *ex*-fiancé—coming to this godforsaken place had more to do with excising the pain and hurt he'd caused, and nothing at all to do with anything new.

But there was a resolution hiding somewhere in her thinking. It went something like '*Get a new life*'. One that didn't involve getting serious with a man and being expected to trust him. Surely that was possible. There had to be plenty of men out there willing to date a well-groomed surgeon with a penchant for fine dining; who didn't want anything other than a good time with no strings.

So why couldn't she raise some enthusiasm for that idea? Because she hadn't got over her last debacle yet. Six months since she'd been dumped, let down badly by the one man who'd told her repeatedly he'd loved and cherished her. Her heart still hadn't recovered from those lies. Or from the humiliation that rankled every time someone at work spoke of how sorry they were to hear about her broken engagement. Of course they were. Sorry they'd missed out on going to her big, fancy wedding, more like.

After learning of the baby *her* fiancé was expecting

with that sweet little nurse working in Recovery, Sarah had
started putting in horrendous hours at the private hospital
where she was a partner. It had been a useless attempt to
numb the agony his infidelity caused her. Not to mention
how she'd exhausted herself so she fell into bed at the end
of each day instead of drumming up painful and nasty
things to do to the man she'd loved.

And it was that man's fault her father had decided, actually insisted, she get away for a few months. What had
really tipped the scales for her in favour of time away from
Auckland was that her ex was due back shortly from his
honeymoon in Paris.

Swiping at the annoying moisture in her eyes, Sarah
pushed aside the image of *her* beautiful French-styled wedding gown still hanging in its cover in the wardrobe of her
spare bedroom.

Why couldn't she forget those damning words her fiancé had uttered as he'd left her apartment for the last time.
*You should never have children. You'd be taking a risk of
screwing up their lives for ever.*

It had been depressingly easy to replace her at work
with an eager young surgeon thrilled to get an opportunity to work in the prestigious surgical hospital her father
had created. And who could blame the guy? Not her. Even
being a little jaded with the endless parade of patients she
saw daily, she still fully understood the power of her father's reputation.

'So here I am.' She sighed. 'Stuck on a narrow strip of
sodden grass beside the coastal highway that leads from
nowhere to nowhere.'

Her Jaguar was copping a pounding from a deluge so
heavy the metalwork would probably be dented when the
rain stopped. If it ever stopped.

Using her forearm to wipe the condensation from the

inside of her window, she peered through the murk. The end of the Jag's bonnet was barely visible, let alone the road she'd crept off to park on the verge. Following the tortuous route along the coast where numerous cliffs fell away to the wild ocean, she'd been terrified of driving over the edge to a watery grave. But staying on the road when she couldn't see a thing had been equally dangerous.

So much for new beginnings. A totally inauspicious start to the year. And she still had to front up to the surgical job she'd agreed to take. Sarah's hands clenched, as they were prone to do these days whenever she wondered what her future held for her. These coming months in Port Weston were an interim measure. This wasn't a place she'd be stopping in for long. Fancy leaving a balmy Auckland to come and spend the summer in one of New Zealand's wettest regions. Yep. A really clever move.

Her father's none-too-gentle arguments aside, the CEO of Port Weston Hospital had been very persuasive, if not a little desperate. He'd needed a general surgeon so that Dr Daniel Reilly could take a long overdue break. A *forced* break, apparently. What sort of man did that make this Reilly character? A workaholic? She shuddered. She knew what they were like, having grown up with one. Or was she an arrogant surgeon who believed no one could replace him? Her ex-fiancé came to mind.

Sharp wind gusts buffeted the heavy car, shaking it alarmingly. Was she destined to spend her three-month contract perched on the top of a cliff face? On the passenger seat lay one half-full bottle of glacial water, a mottled banana and two day-old fruit muffins that had looked dubious when she'd bought them back at some one-store town with a forgettable name. Not a lot of food to survive on if this storm didn't hurry up and pass through.

Sarah returned to staring out the window. Was it raining

in Paris? She hoped so. Then she blinked. And craned her neck forward. There was the road she'd abandoned half an hour ago. And the edge of the precipice she'd parked on—less than two metres from the nose of her car. A chill slid down her spine, her mouth dried. Her eyes bulged in disbelief at how close she'd come to plummeting down to the sea.

With the rain easing, she could hear the wild crash of waves on the rocks below. Reaching for the ignition, she suddenly hesitated. It might be wise to check her situation before backing onto the road.

Outside the car she shivered and tugged her jacket closer to her body. A quick lap around the vehicle showed no difficulties with returning to the road. Then voices reached her. Shouts, cries, words—snatched away by the wind.

Pushing one foot forward cautiously, then the other, she moved ever closer to the cliff edge. As she slowly leaned forward and peered gingerly over the side, her heart thumped against her ribs. The bank dropped directly down to the ocean-licked rocks.

More shouts. From the left. Sarah steeled herself for another look. Fifty metres away, on a rock-strewn beach, people clustered at the water's edge, dicing with the treacherous waves crashing around their feet and tugging them off balance. Her survey of the scene stopped at one dark-haired man standing further into the sea, hands on hips. From this angle it was impossible to guess his height, but his shoulders were impressive. Her interest quickened. He seemed focused on one particular spot in the water.

Trying to follow the direction of his gaze, she saw a boat bouncing against the waves as it pushed out to sea at an achingly slow pace. She gasped. Beyond the waves floated a person—face down.

Happy New Year.

* * *

Daniel Reilly stood knee-deep in the roiling water, his heart in his throat as the rescuers tried to navigate the charging waves. Aboard their boat lay an injured person. Alive or dead, Dan didn't know, but *he'd* have a cardiac arrest soon if these incredibly brave—and foolhardy—men didn't get back on land before someone else was lost.

The whole situation infuriated him. If only people would read the wretched signs and take heed. They weren't put there for fun. It was bad enough having two people missing in the sea, a father and son according to the police. It would be totally stupid if one of the volunteer rescuers drowned while searching for them.

'Doc, get back up the beach. We'll bring him to you,' a rescuer yelled at him. 'It's the lad, Anders Starne.'

'He doesn't look too good,' Pat O'Connor, the local constable, called over the din.

Like the middle-aged cop, Dan had seen similar tragedies all too often around here. It wasn't known as a wild, unforgiving coastline for nothing. But most calamities could be avoided if people used their brains. His hands gripped his hips as he cursed under his breath.

The kid had better be alive. Though Dan didn't like the chances, it was inherent in him to believe there was life still beating in a body until proven otherwise.

Waterlogged men laid Anders on the sand, a teenager with his life ahead of him. Dan's gut clenched as he thought of his own daughter. Even at four she pushed all the boundaries, and Dan couldn't begin to imagine how he'd cope with a scenario like this. He totally understood why the father had leapt off the rocks in a vain attempt to save his son. *He* would do anything if Leah's life was in jeopardy.

'Except take a long break to spend time with her.' The annoying voice of one of his closest friends, and boss, resonated in his head.

Yeah, well, he was doing his best. And because of interference from the board's chairman, Charlie Drummond, he *was* taking time off, starting tomorrow. Pity Charlie couldn't tell him how he was supposed to entertain his daughter, because he sure didn't have a clue. Hopscotch and finger puppets were all very well, but for twelve weeks? What if he got it all wrong again? He'd be back at the beginning with Leah an emotional mess and he distraught from not knowing how to look after his girl. That scared him witless. He focused on the boy lying on the beach. Far easier.

Dropping to his knees, he tore at the boy's clothing, his fingers touching cold skin in their search for a carotid pulse. A light, yet steady, throbbing under his fingers lifted his mood. He smiled up at the silent crowd of locals surrounding him. 'He's alive.'

'Excuse me. Let me through. I'm a doctor.' A lilting, female voice intruded on Dan's concentration.

Annoyed at the disturbance, he flicked a look up at the interloper. 'That makes two of us,' he snapped, and returned his attention to his patient. But not before he saw a vision of a shapely female frame looming over him. *Very* shapely.

'Where'd you come from?' he demanded as he explored Anders's head with his fingers.

'Does that matter at this moment?' she retorted.

'Not really.' He was local and therefore in charge.

'What have you found so far?' She, whoever she was, knelt on the other side of the boy.

He was aware of her scrutinising him. 'His pulse is steady.' He was abrupt with her as he straightened and looked her in the eye. Her gaze slammed into him, shocking the air out of his lungs. Eyes as green as the bush-clad hills behind them. And as compelling.

'Then he's one very lucky boy.' Her tone so reasonable it was irritating.

And intriguing. Who was she? He'd never seen her before, and she wasn't someone he'd easily forget with that elegant stance and striking face. He shook his head. Right now he didn't need to know anything about her.

Jerking his gaze away, he spoke to the crowd again, 'Someone get my bag from my truck. Fast.' To the doctor—how did she distract him so easily?—he said, 'I'll wrap him in a survival blanket to prevent any more loss of body heat.'

The kid coughed. Spewed salt water. Together they rolled him onto his side, water oozing out the corner of his mouth as he continued coughing. His eyelids dragged open, then drooped shut.

'Here, Dan.' Malcolm, his brother and the head of the local search and rescue crew, pushed through the crowd to drop a bag in the sand. Dan snapped open the catches and delved into the bag for tissues and the foil blanket.

'Thanks.' The other doctor flicked the tissues from his grasp. Dan squashed his admiration for her efficiency watching her cleaning the boy's mouth and chin as she tenderly checked his bruised face simultaneously. Her long, slim fingers tipped with pale rose-coloured polish were thorough in their survey.

'I don't think the cheek bones are fractured.' Her face tilted up, and her eyes met his.

Again her gaze slammed into him, taking his breath away. The same relief he felt for the boy was reflected in her eyes. Facial bones were delicate and required the kind of surgical procedures he wasn't trained to perform. He gave her a thumbs-up. 'Thank goodness.'

The rain returned, adding to the boy's discomfort. Dan began rolling Anders gently one way, then the other, tuck-

ing him into the blanket, at the same time checking for
injuries. He found deep gashes on Anders's back and one
arm lay at an odd angle, undoubtedly fractured. For now
the wounds weren't bleeding, no doubt due to the low body
temperature, but as that rose the haemorrhaging would
start. The deep gash above one eyebrow would be the
worst.

'Where's the ambulance?' Dan asked Pat.

'On its way. About three minutes out. It was held up by
a slip at Black's Corner.'

Anger shook Dan once more. This boy's life could've
indirectly been jeopardised because of some officious idiot's unsound reasoning. For years now the locals had been
petitioning to get Black's Corner straightened and the un-
stable hillside bulldozed away, but the council didn't have
a lot of funds and small towns like Port Weston missed
out all the time. He'd be making a phone call to the mayor
later.

Looking down at the boy, Dan asked, 'Anders, can you
hear me?' Eyelids flickered, which Dan took for a yes.
'You've been in an accident. A wave swept you off the
rocks. I'm checking for broken bones. Okay?'

Dan didn't expect an answer. He didn't get one. He
wasn't sure if the boy could hear clearly or was just re-
sponding to any vocal sounds, so he kept talking. It must
be hellishly frightening for Anders to be surrounded by
strangers while in pain and freezing cold.

Beneath the thermal blanket Dan felt the boy's abdo-
men. No hard swelling to indicate internal bleeding. The
spleen felt normal. So far so good. But the sooner this boy
was in hospital the better.

'That left arm doesn't look right,' a knowledgeable, and
sensual, feminine voice spoke across the boy.

Dan's fingers worked at the point where the arm twisted

under Anders's body. His nod was terse. 'Compound fracture, and dislocated shoulder.'

'Are we going to pop that shoulder back in place now?'

'We should. Otherwise the time frame will be too long and he might require surgery.'

'I'll hold him for you.' No questions, no time wasting. She trusted him to get on with it.

Daniel appreciated anyone who trusted his judgement, or anything about him, come to that. His mouth twisted sideways as he slid the boy's tattered shirt away from his shoulder. 'A shot of morphine will make him more comfortable.'

The drug quickly took effect. Dan raised the arm and, using all his strength, rotated the head of the humerus, popping the ball joint back into its socket. Sweat beaded on his forehead.

The woman lifted Anders's upper body while Dan wound a crepe bandage around the shoulder to hold it in place temporarily. As they worked, a whiff of her exotic perfume tantalised him, brought memories of another fragrance, another woman. His wife. She'd always worn perfume, even when mucking out the horses.

'Where's that ambulance?' He was brusque, annoyed at the painful images conjured up in his mind by a darned scent.

Warmth touched his face, and so distracted had he been that it took a moment to realise that it was the sun. A quick look around showed the clouds had rolled back and once again the beach was sparkling as it bathed in the yellow light. Things were looking up.

As though reading his mind, Pat said, 'Now that the rain has moved up the coast, the helicopter will be on its way. That'll make our search a little easier.'

The boy's father. Dan's stomach clenched as he looked

up at Pat, saw the imperceptible shake of the cop's head in answer to his unspoken question. Deep sadness gripped him. Time was running out to find the man alive.

'It was sheer chance the men found the lad when they did.' Even as Pat talked they heard the deep sound of rotors beating in the air.

'Hey, Daniel,' a familiar voice called. Kerry was a local volunteer ambulance officer. 'What've we got?'

Dan quickly filled him in and within moments Anders was being ferried on a stretcher to the ambulance. There went one very lucky boy. Dan watched the vehicle pull away, thinking about the waves throwing a body onto the sharp jags of the rocks. He shivered abruptly.

'What happened out there?' The woman stood beside him, nodding towards the sea.

Dan shook the image from his head and turned to face this other distraction. His world tilted as he once more looked into those fathomless eyes. It was hard to focus on answering her question. 'Anders and his father were fishing off the rocks—'

'In this weather? That's crazy,' she interrupted.

'Of course it's crazy.' His jaw tightened. 'But it happens. Anders slipped and his father leapt in after him.'

'And the father's still missing.' It was a soft statement of fact. Her eyes were directed to the sea, scanning the horizon.

'I'm afraid so.' He lightened his tone. 'Thank you for your help. You happened along at exactly the right moment.' He wouldn't thank her for the unwelcome hollow feeling in his gut that had started when this perturbing woman had arrived. Or the sensation of something missing from his life that he hadn't been aware of until now. Soon she'd be on her way and then he'd forget this silly, unwelcome impression she'd made.

'You can thank the appalling weather for that. I'd pulled off the road, and when the rain cleared I saw you all down here.'

His eyes scanned the close horizon. Already the sun was disappearing behind a veil of clouds. 'Looks like we're in for more.'

'When doesn't it rain?' Exasperation tightened her face.

'If it's not raining around here that's because it either just stopped or is about to start.' In reality it wasn't all that bad, but why destroy the coast's reputation for bad weather? Especially with someone just passing through. Weird how that notion suddenly saddened him. Odd that a complete stranger had rocked him, reminding him of things he'd deliberately forgotten for years.

A sudden, unexpected thought slammed into his brain. Maybe it was time to start dating again. Like when? If he didn't have time for his daughter, how would he manage fitting another person into his life? He couldn't. End of story. End of stupid ideas.

The woman's tight smile was still in place as her hands wiped at her damp jacket. 'Guess we just had a fine spell, then.'

'At least you got to see it.' He mustered a joke, and was rewarded with a light laugh. A carefree tinkle that hovered in the air between them, drew him closer to her, wound an invisible thread around them both.

Then she glanced down at her feet and grimaced with disgust as she noticed the sloppy, glue-like mud that coated her pretty sandals. He'd swear she shuddered. Definitely a city dweller. Nothing like the women he knew and loved: wholesome, country women like his sisters and his late wife.

Trying to sound sympathetic, he said, 'You should've worn gumboots.'

'Gumboots?' Those carefully crafted eyebrows rose with indignation.

'Yes. Rubber boots that reach the tops of your shins.'

'I know what gumboots are.'

Bet she'd never worn them. 'Sure you do.'

'Do you suppose I might be able to get a designer pair?'

'Possum fur around the tops?' Keep it light, then send her on her way before he did something dumb, like offer her coffee.

She tilted her head to one side. 'How about crochet daisies? Yellow, to contrast with the black rubber.'

'Hey, Dan, you heading to the hospital?' Pat called across the sand.

Thankful for the interruption, Dan shook his head. 'No, Alison can take care of the lad. I'll hang around in case the guys find Starne senior.' He patted his belt, checking for his pager.

'Who's Alison?' the woman beside him asked.

'She's in charge of the emergency department and has a surgical background. She'd call if she needs me.' *What does this have to do with you? You're an outsider.*

'Do you mind if I wait a while with you?'

Yes, I do. Inexplicably he wanted her gone. As though a safety mechanism was warning him to get away from her before it was too late.

Yet he couldn't prevent his head turning towards her. Blonde strands of hair whipped across her cheeks in the skittish wind. He let his gaze wander over her. She was designer from head to foot. Her jacket was soft suede. Her well-fitted trousers had not come off a rack, at least not any ordinary shop rack. But what really caught his interest were the long, shapely legs those wet trousers clung to. They went on for ever.

'Pardon? Oh, sorry. You want to stay? It's not necessary.' Flustered at having been sidetracked, he tripped over his words. First she had him joking with her, then she addled his brain. He struggled to focus on the important issues, not her. 'If the searchers find anything now, it's more likely to be a body. No one can survive in that icy water for very long.'

'True, but it's hard to give up hope, isn't it?' Her eyes were enormous in her pale face.

'Very hard.' His stomach tightened, because of the sad and pointless waste of a life. Not because of the empathy in her eyes.

'I'd still like to wait.' She wasn't asking him, she was telling him, quietly but firmly.

Then from left field he felt a stirring in a region of his body he'd thought long dead. For two despair-filled years, he'd been unintentionally celibate. Now he couldn't help himself—he glanced down at his groin. Relief poured through him. His reaction had been small. Tipping his head back, he laughed. Another long-forgotten act.

Definitely time to get out and about. That new nurse in the neonatal unit had dropped enough hints, and she obviously liked babies if she worked with them, which had to be a plus. Leah needed siblings. He'd never wanted her to be an only child.

He rubbed his arms. Wanting more children had led to a load of stress and difficulties in his otherwise wonderful marriage. Family was so important. Look how his sisters and brother had rallied round when Celine had died. But Leah would miss out on so much if he didn't rectify the situation soon. Dating meant getting involved with another person. Was he ready? Would he ever be ready? Not while his guilt over letting down Celine hung over him like a dirty cloud.

Their marriage had been cut short by an aneurysm.

Cut short before they could resolve their problems. The shock of finding Celine's lifeless body in the bathroom, with Leah sitting beside her singing as though nothing was wrong, still rocked Dan when he thought about it.

Which was why he didn't think about it.

That's also why dating was a bad idea. The whole concept of having someone else he might care about taken away from him so abruptly sent him into a cold sweat.

Suddenly the unknown woman thrust a hand out. 'By the way, I'm Sarah Livingston, your replacement surgeon.'

'Stone the crows.' Shock barrelled through him.

It hadn't occurred to him she might be the locum they expected to arrive tomorrow. The idea was absurd. She was too citified to be stopping here. Too…different. She wouldn't fit in at all. His stomach tightened another notch. So she wasn't passing through.

She was moving in.

Into his hospital, his clinic. Into his house.

Sarah tensed. What did the guy mean? *Stone the crows.* Hadn't she just performed in a capable and professional manner? 'You've got a problem with me?'

'Ahh, no.' The man sounded flummoxed. 'Not at all.'

'I didn't try to take control of your accident scene.' Which was unusual. She hated playing second fiddle to anyone. But in this circumstance she'd gone along with him without any concerns. Odd. Was she coming down with something?

So far her impressions of him were straightforward. Strong hands. Sopping-wet, longish hair that appeared black. Eyes that held a load of caution and a quick anger. Then there were those wide shoulders that V'd down to narrow hips. He totally lacked style—his jeans and the baggy, woollen overshirt under his jacket were way past their use-by date. On a professional note, which was far more important, he'd performed very competently with the boy.

'You certainly made things easier for me.' His voice was deep, gruff, reminding her of a thistle—rough and prickly exterior, soft inside.

'You are Dr Daniel Reilly? I heard someone call you Dan so I presumed so. If I'm mistaken, I'm sorry.'

His handshake was firm but brief, as though glad to get the niceties over. But not so fast that she didn't notice the electricity flaring between them at his touch. Heat sizzled across her palm. Deep in her tummy warmth unfurled, reached throughout her body, reddened her cheeks.

'It's my practice you'll be looking after.' His tone hardened.

So that was it. He wasn't happy about leaving his practice in someone else's hands. The reluctance came through loud and clear. So why had he been told to take a break?

'I thought you'd be pleased to see me, eager to get on with your holiday.' She swallowed her disappointment at his lack of welcome. At least with him going on leave she mightn't see much of him. She hoped.

Really? Truly? You don't want to follow up on this attraction for him that's gripping you? Absolutely not. Too soon after Oliver's betrayal. Who said anything about getting close? What about a fling? A sigh slipped across her bottom lip as she studied Dr Reilly. She doubted her ability to have an affair and not get a little bit close to him. What a shame.

He ignored her jibe, instead turning his back to the pounding surf and nodding at an old, weatherboard building on the other side of the road. 'We'll wait in the Gold Miners' Pub. Can't have you catching a chill.'

As if. Sarah looked around at the sodden beach, the

black, churning waters of the Tasman Sea, the heavy, leaden clouds racing in. Everything was wet, wet, wet. How could she have thought leaving home would help put the last few months behind her? She could've decided about her future in an environment she was used to, not on an alien planet.

How stupid to think doing a complete flip-over of her life would change anything. She shoved her fists into her jacket pockets, already knowing she should've stayed at home for these months, should've told her father no. Right now she'd be in her gorgeous apartment overlooking Auckland's inner harbour, the vibrant City of Sails, where money talked. Where gorgeous, chic sandals stayed gorgeous, not getting ruined the moment she hopped out of her car.

The months in Port Weston stretched out before her like an endless road. But she wasn't quitting. Port Weston might be like nothing she was used to, but she had to stay. She'd given her word.

Then her eyes focused on Daniel Reilly, and for some unknown reason she wondered if she'd be wise to leave right away, while she still could.

CHAPTER TWO

DR REILLY made Sarah, at five feet six, feel almost short. Following him into the dark, wood-panelled interior of the Gold Miners' Pub, she admired his easy, smooth gait, his natural grace that belied his big build. The latent strength she'd glimpsed when he'd popped Anders's joint back was evident in the set of his shoulders, in the loose swing of his hands. Her tongue licked her lips. Gorgeous.

He turned to her. 'A shot of something strong will warm you through and stop your teeth chattering.'

'I'd prefer Earl Grey tea.'

He winced. 'Earl Grey? On the Coast?' His eyes rolled. 'That fancy city stuff won't win you many friends around here.'

'As that's not why I'm here, it doesn't matter.'

'I'd like a practice to return to.'

'Not a problem.' The man's looks might take her breath away but his prickly disposition annoyed her. Was she the only one he treated that way? Probably not, if he had to be forced to take leave. The intensity with which he studied her sent a blush right down to her toes. Did he like what he saw? Did she care? Uh, hello? Unbelievable how quickly her awareness of him had reached the point where she wondered how his touch on her skin would affect her. It would burn her up, she suspected. Her overreaction must be due to the contrast between the overly hot room and the chilly dampness outside. What else could it be?

Try lust or physical attraction; forget the weather. Really? Then her stomach growled. That's what this was all about. Lack of food. Not Dr Yummy.

'I heard that grumbling,' the man dominating her thoughts said, amusement briefly lightening those cool, assessing eyes.

'I'm starving.' Hardly surprising. Unable to bring herself to eat those woeful muffins, her last meal had been breakfast. A glance at her watch showed it was now after five.

Behind the long bar a pretty woman with wild red hair called across the room. 'Dan, the hospital phoned to say everything's under control.' The woman looked pointedly at Sarah. 'Can I get you both a drink? I'm sure your friend might like something.'

Shock registered on Dan's face. 'This is Sarah Livingston. My locum.'

Not his friend. Probably never would be. What a pity.

'Are you really?' the woman asked Sarah, her face lighting up with a speculative gleam as her gaze moved to Dan and back. 'Wonderful.'

Sarah gulped. Don't get any bright ideas about matchmaking. If Oliver's defection had taught her anything it was not to trust as easily as she had last time. Besides, Dan Reilly was far too unsophisticated for her liking. Except that sculpted body did fascinate her. Maybe she could cope with unsophisticated—as an interlude. Hadn't she thought about having fun with men who didn't want anything more demanding? But an affair with this man? Not likely. That could complicate things when she had to step into his shoes at the local hospital.

Dan continued the introductions. 'Jill's our head theatre nurse, and a barmaid in her spare time. She'll get you whatever you want, though a slug of brandy would do you a sight more good than tea.'

Sarah retorted, 'Suggestion noted.' Forget the interlude. If she ever progressed to having an affair it would be with someone personable and fun, not grumpy and domineering.

Jill leaned across the counter. 'Welcome to Port Weston. Since we'll be working together, give me a call if you have any questions about work or anything else. Or if you're ever hankering for a coffee, I'm available.'

'Thanks for that.' At least someone was pleased to see her here. 'You must be busy, with two jobs.'

'Malcolm, my husband and Dan's brother, runs the pub except when he's out rescuing fools who don't read warning signs.' Jill banged two glasses on the counter. 'What'll it be?'

'Two brandies.' Dan didn't consult Sarah, instead told her, 'Malcolm's the search and rescue coordinator.'

'He was one of the men who'd carried Anders in?' No wonder Jill looked worried.

'Yep.' Dan sipped his drink appreciatively.

'I'll bet he went straight back out to sea after handing his charge over to you.' Jill glared at Dan.

'Hey, steady up. You know there's no way I could've stopped him. A team of Clydesdale horses couldn't have.' Dan reached across and covered Jill's hand with his.

There were tears in the other woman's eyes. 'I know, but he worries me silly. One day he won't come back from a rescue mission.'

Sarah found herself wanting to hug Jill. And she didn't do hugs. Not very often anyway. Certainly not with people she'd only just met. But, then, she wasn't normally rattled by a man like Dan either. Or any man, come to think of it. Must be something in the West Coast air.

Dan said to Jill, 'Don't think like that. You know you wouldn't change him for anything.' Then he turned his attention back to Sarah. 'We'd better get out of our wet clothes. You're shivering non-stop.'

'I'll get some dry things from my car in a moment.' Sarah took a large swallow of brandy, gasping as it burned a track down her throat. 'Wow.'

'Wait till the warmth spreads through you, then you won't be twisting your nose sideways like that.' Dan actually smiled. A long, slow smile that at last went all the way to his eyes.

Blue eyes. So what? It was a common colour. But other blue eyes didn't remind her of hot, lazy days at the beach. Or make her toes curl up in anticipation of exciting things to come. Like what? Who cared? Anything with this man would be exhilarating. Was it possible to become drunk in thirty seconds? Because that's how she felt.

'Where're your keys? I'll get your bag, save you getting another drenching.'

So he could do 'nice'. She dug into her jacket pocket, handed her keyring to him. 'My car's out the front.'

His fingers were warm against hers as he took the keys. 'I know. It's the odd one out amongst the dirty four–wheel-drives and family wagons.'

'It fits in where I come from.'

'I'm sure it does.' Dan hauled the heavy front door open with a jerk. 'Malcolm still hasn't shaved this blasted door, Jill.'

'Tell him, not me.' Jill topped up Sarah's glass even though it wasn't empty. 'Here, a bit more won't hurt you. There's no colour in your cheeks.'

'Thanks, but I'd better go easy on it.' What she really needed was food.

'A hot shower will do you wonders. You can use our bathroom.'

A blast of cold air hit her as Dan poked his head around the door, looking bemused. 'Which bag?'

'The small one.' Hopefully that contained everything she needed.

'You didn't bring a small one,' Dan retorted. 'Why do some women have to cart their whole wardrobe everywhere they go?'

'Guess that's a rhetorical question.' Sarah stared at the closing door.

'Guess he's exaggerating?' Jill's smile warmed her.

'Definitely not *all* my clothes.' Already she liked Jill enough to relax with her. Could she be making a new friend? What was the point? She'd be gone in three months. There again, a friend would be good. She missed the three women she'd known since high school and done all her growing up with.

They'd gone to university together, coming out well versed in life and clutching degrees to their proud chests. Two doctors, one architect and an advertising guru. Three marriages, three mothers; and then there was her. Sometimes she knew she didn't quite belong to the quartet any more. Conversations over dinners and coffee seemed to revolve around children and school timetables, husbands and schedules—things Sarah didn't have a clue about.

Jill was still talking. 'Dan's okay behind that rugged exterior. A pussy cat really. You'll get along fine.'

Sarah knew pussycats, even those in disguise. Dan didn't fit the bill. Tiger was a more apt description. Stealthy when he had to be. Fast when he went for the kill. There was a mix of strength and stubbornness in the set of his chin. His classic handsome features were made interesting by a too-wide mouth and a ragged scar on the point of his chin.

'Here you go, the small one,' Dan said from behind her, causing her to jump. Definitely stealthy.

Jill asked Dan, 'Can you show Sarah to my bedroom? The rescue crew can't be far away and they'll be wanting food.'

At the mention of food Sarah's stomach turned over. 'I'll be as quick as I can, and then I'll give you a hand,' she told Jill. Whoa, back up. She'd help? In a pub? She'd get messy and greasy.

New year, new life, remember?

'Along here.' Dan led the way out to the back and into the private quarters. He opened a door and let her precede him into a double bedroom. 'The bathroom's through there.'

He smelt of damp wool and warm male as she brushed past him. No trace of expensive aftershave or hair product. A clean, uninhibited masculine scent. Sarah hesitated, looked back over her shoulder at him, a sudden longing for something she couldn't put her finger on gripping her.

'What about you?' She was suddenly, oddly, nervous.

Placing her case in the middle of the floor, he turned to leave. His look was cool, his mouth a straight line. 'There's another bathroom next door.'

As she poked through her case for suitable clothes she could hear Dan moving about in that other bathroom, presumably preparing for his shower. An image of a well-muscled body filled her mind. And of a rare but endearing, smile tinged with sadness. What caused that sadness? Of course, she could be wrong about the muscles. She hoped not. A thrill of pleasure warmed her body—and shook her carefully formulated concept of her time in Port Weston.

The jets of water were piping hot against her skin and she gave herself up to them, putting aside thoughts of Daniel Reilly, good and otherwise. Especially those about his body. But how could a bad-tempered man wearing such shapeless clothes ooze so much sex appeal?

The bar was crowded and the mood sombre when Sarah returned. Dan was perched on a stool at the end of the long counter. He waved her over. 'Do you want another drink?'

Schooling her face into a smile, Sarah looked him over as she replied, 'No, thanks.'

His clean shirt fitted snugly across his chest while his dry, worn jeans were tight. Her mouth dried. Beneath the faded denim his thighs were every bit as muscular as she'd imagined.

'Anders's father still hasn't been found.'

'That's not good.' She pulled her shoulders back, focusing on what Dan said, not what he wore.

'That lad needs his father alive and well, not dead and washed up on a beach,' Dan snapped.

'Some people will always take chances.' But not her. She'd focused on her career, foregoing a relationship until she'd specialised, at the same time working on making her father proud.

'They shouldn't, not when they've got a family to consider.'

Sarah totally agreed with him, but diplomatically changed the subject. 'Does Port Weston have a GP? I didn't see one on the beach.'

'Tony Blowers. He's up a valley, delivering a baby, at the moment.'

'Lucky for Anders you were here, then.' She looked around, spied Jill busy pulling beers, and remembered her promise. 'I said I'd help with the food so I'd better find out what's to be done.'

'You did?' He didn't bother disguising his surprise. Those intense cobalt eyes measured her up and down, making her very aware of the snug black slacks and black figure-hugging cotton sweater she'd pulled on.

Dan drawled, 'You might just fit in here yet.'

Pity he didn't sound like he meant it. 'You don't want me here, do you?'

'No, I don't.'

'Thank you for your honesty.' *That* she could deal with. It was a little harder to ignore the fact he wouldn't give her a chance.

'It's nothing personal,' Dan added quietly.

'That's a relief,' she muttered, hoping he meant it and wasn't trying to placate her.

The door crashed back against the wall and drenched men, carrying a stretcher, pressed into the pub. Pat told Dan, 'We've found Starne. He washed up further along and tried to climb the cliff. Fell, and broke his arm, by the look of it.'

'Put him on the couch. It's warmer in here than in a bedroom.' Dan removed cushions and the men lowered the stretcher.

Kneeling down beside the man, Sarah told him, 'I'm Sarah Livingston, a doctor. Can you hear me?'

The man's eyes flew open. 'Where's my son? Is he all right?' He tried sitting up, pushing on his elbows, only to flop back down, groaning with pain.

Dan laid a hand on the man's chest. 'Take it easy.'

Starne tried to knock Dan's hand away with his good arm. 'Is my boy all right? Tell me what happened to him.' The distressed man looked ready to leap up off the couch.

'I'm Dan Reilly, a surgeon. I saw Anders when the rescuers brought him onto the beach.' Dan continued giving Starne the details about his boy, finishing with, 'He's in hospital and doing well.'

Jill helped Sarah tuck blankets around the man. 'I'll have hot-water bottles ready very soon.'

Tears streamed down the man's face. 'The waves banged Anders against the rocks so many times. I couldn't reach him. I thought he was gone.'

'You're both very lucky.' Sarah noted his pulse rate as she talked.

Dan nudged her, spoke softly. 'You're doing great with him, calming him down better than I managed. I'll do the secondary survey.'

She nodded, pleased with the compliment, however small, and silently counted the rise and fall of their patient's chest. 'I'm onto the resps.'

As his fingers felt for contusions Dan told their patient, 'I'll check you over, starting with your head.'

Those firm, gently probing fingers on Starnes's scalp tantalised her. What would they be like on her skin, stroking, teasing, racking up the tension? 'Damn.' She started counting again.

Dan glanced at Sarah as he worked. 'The sooner we get this man to hospital where he can see his boy, the better. I know that's what I'd want if I'd been thinking the worst.'

Sarah's heart squeezed. No parent wanted to outlive their child. As hers had done. 'The downside of being a parent.'

She hadn't realised she'd spoken aloud until Dan said, 'Children cause a lot of worry and heartache, that's for sure. Have you got any?'

'No.'

'I guess now's not the time to ask why not.'

There'd never be a right time. 'Resps slightly slow.'

'Temperature?' Dan asked. At least he could take a hint.

Sarah looked around for Jill. 'You wouldn't have a thermometer?'

'Coming up.' Jill was already halfway out the room.

'Finding anything?' Dan asked Sarah as she palpated Starnes's stomach and liver.

She shook her head. 'These two should buy a lottery ticket.'

'We're certainly not giving you time to settle in quietly, are we?' Dan looked at her for a moment.

No, and being so close to him, breathing his very maleness, added to the sense of walking a swaying tightrope. 'Guess I'll manage,' she muttered, not sure whether she meant the patients or Dan.

Someone handed them hot-water bottles, Sarah reaching for them at the same moment as Dan. Their hands touched, fingers curled around each other's before they could untwine themselves. 'S-sorry.' Sarah snatched her hand back.

'No problem,' snapped Dan, his eyes wide and his face still.

Sarah cringed. Did he think she'd done that on purpose? Surely not? She couldn't deny her attraction for him, but to deliberately grab his hand when she hardly knew him was not her style. Knowing that to say anything in her defence would only make the situation worse, she kept quiet, and again reached for the bottles, making sure to keep well away from Dan.

She placed the bottles in Starnes's armpits and around his groin to maximise his potential for absorbing the warmth.

'The left ankle is swollen, possibly sprained,' Sarah pointed.

'My thoughts exactly.'

'Will we—I—be required to go into theatre if surgery's needed?' Sarah almost hoped not. She was tired and hungry, not in good shape to be operating.

Dan sat back on his haunches and those piercing eyes clashed with hers. 'You don't officially start until tomorrow so if someone's needed I'll do it.'

Why? She'd come for one reason only, and he was holding her back. As her blood started heating up and her tongue forming a sharp reply, he continued, 'You'll want to unpack and settle in at the house. Alison should manage unless she's got another emergency.'

Sarah eased off on her annoyance. How could she stay mad when those eyes bored into her like hot summer rays? 'As long as you know I'm happy to assist if needed.'

A blast of cold air announced the arrival of the ambulance crew. 'Hi, there, again.' Kerry hunkered down beside Dan. 'What've we got this time?'

While Dan relayed the details Sarah stood and stretched her calf muscles, arching her back and pulling her shoulders taut. Dan's gaze followed her movements as he talked to the paramedic, sending a thrill through her. Those eyes seemed to cruise over her, as though they could see right through her to things she never told anyone. Which was plain crazy. How could this man, a stranger really, see through her façade? See beyond the clothes to her soul? He couldn't. Could he?

'Here...' Jill waved across the punters' heads. 'Sandwiches and a coffee. Or would you like something stronger?'

'Coffee's fine.' Grateful for the food, Sarah swallowed her disappointment at the mug of murky instant coffee being slid across the counter towards her. 'Do you still need a hand in the kitchen?'

'I've got it covered. Bea arrived while you were in the

shower, and she's happy as a kid in a sandpit out there cooking up fries.'

'Bea?'

'Dan's sister.'

'Is everyone around here related to him?' Biting into a thick sandwich filled with ham and tomato, Sarah told her stomach to be patient, sustenance was on the way down.

'Not quite.' Dan sent Jill a silent message before turning to Sarah. 'You want to share those?' He nodded at the sandwiches.

Not really. She could eat the lot. 'Sure.' Sarah prodded the plate along the counter towards him, wondering what he hadn't wanted Jill to mention in front of her. 'So you come from a big family.'

'Yep, and they're quite useful at times.'

'What he means is we all run round after him most of the time.' Jill winked at Sarah.

They needn't think she'd play that game. She'd come to run his clinic, nothing else. 'How far from here is the house I'm staying in? I've got some directions but it's probably quicker if you tell me.'

Wariness filtered into Dan's eyes. 'You can follow me shortly.'

'I'd really like to go now.'

'Soon.' Then suddenly his eyes twinkled and he waved at someone behind her. 'Sweetheart, there you are.'

Disappointment jolted Sarah. Of course Dan would have a wife. No man as good looking as this one would be single. Turning to see who he was smiling at, her heart slowed and a lump blocked her throat. The most gorgeous little girl bounded past her, her arms flung high and wide as she reached Dan.

'Daddy, there you are. Auntie Bea brought me here. She made me some fries.'

'Hi, sweetheart. Guess you won't be needing dinner now.' Dan scooped the pink and yellow bundle up and sat her on his knee.

'You're late, Daddy.'

'Sorry, sweetheart.' The man looked unhappy, as though he'd slipped up somehow. 'I had to help Uncle Malcolm.'

Sarah stared at father and daughter. Their eyes were the same shade of blue. They had identical wide, full mouths, the only difference being the little girl's was one big smile while Dan's rarely got past a scowl. Except now, with his daughter in his arms. The lump blocking Sarah's throat slowly evaporated, her heart resumed its normal rhythm. But she melted inside, watching the child.

Since when did children do that to her? Since her wrecked marriage plans had stolen her dream of having a family. Why hadn't Oliver taken that test for the cystic fibrosis gene as he'd promised to do when she'd first told him she was a carrier? Had he been afraid he might find he was imperfect? Did the idea that they might have to decide whether to have children or not if he'd tested positive prove too hard to face? Whatever the answers, he could've talked to her, not gone off and played around behind her back.

'Hello.'

Sarah blinked, looked around, caught the eye of Dan, and, remembering where she was, immediately shoved the past aside. 'Hi.'

The child wriggled around on Dan's knee until she was staring at Sarah. 'Are you the lady who's coming to stay with us?'

Definitely not. 'No, I'm Sarah, a doctor like your father.'

'Sarah…' Dan eased a breath through his teeth. 'Leah's right. You are staying with us.'

'What?' Absolutely not. No one had ever mentioned such a notion. Perspiration broke out on her forehead. Had she missed something? No, she couldn't have. Staying with the local surgeon would've been one detail she'd definitely not overlook. 'The board arranged a hospital house for me.'

'That's right. The one and only hospital house. Where I live with my daughter.'

Her shoulders sagged. He meant it. She was staying at Dan's house. With Dan. And his daughter. 'Your wife?'

'There's just the two of us.' His mouth tightened. 'You'll be comfortable enough.'

No way. She couldn't, wouldn't. What about her unprecedented attraction to him? How could she handle that when they were squeezed into the same place? Then there was the job. He'd always be asking how she was doing. Who had she seen? How was she treating them? Her voice sounded shrill even to her. 'There must be somewhere else. I don't mind a small flat or apartment.'

'This is Port Weston, not Auckland. Rental properties are few and far between. When I say there's nothing else then there's nothing. Believe me, I've checked.' Dan stood up. 'I'm not happy about it either. Unfortunately we're going to have to bump along together—somehow.'

Of course Dan didn't want her staying with him. He didn't want her here, full stop. Tiredness dragged her shoulders down as she stood up from the stool she'd been perched on. 'I'll get my case.'

Bump along together, indeed. Her eyes widened and her face heated up. In a fantasy world, bumping up against Dan might be a whole heap of fun. There were definitely some very intriguing ways. But not in the ho-hum kind of way he was suggesting. Right now she wanted to bang him over the head for letting this happen.

* * *

Swinging Leah down to the floor, Dan watched Sarah striding across the room in a second, clean pair of silly sandals. Her cheeks had coloured up, and her shoulders were stiff. Those amazing eyes were giving off sparks. Passion ran through her veins, he'd bet his job on it.

'Sarah's unhappy, Daddy.' Leah wriggled down to the floor and grabbed his hand.

So was he. He didn't need a sex siren in his home. Not when his body suddenly seemed to be waking up. But he couldn't be blamed for the board crying off outlaying money for separate accommodation for her. It was part of his tenancy agreement that visiting doctors stayed with him. Of course, none of them came for more than a week at a time.

Charlie had also stressed the importance of keeping Dr Livingston happy during her time here. *And then they put her in with me?* Dan bit off an expletive.

Everyone in the district knew that Dr Livingston had to be looked out for. There'd be a concerted effort to make sure she wanted for nothing. The board had a plan. One where the locum would fall in love with Port Weston and its hospital and want to stay on when the contract was up. The plan was doomed from the start. By all appearances Sarah would not stay one minute longer than her contract stated. But the relief that knowledge should engender within him wasn't forthcoming.

Did he want her to stay? No.

Did he want to cut back his working hours permanently? Maybe. If it all worked out with Leah. If he learned how to give her what she needed and didn't fail her like he had last time he'd tried to be a hands-on solo dad. If. If. If.

Then he had to think about those little mistakes he'd begun making at work because he'd become exhausted. Thankfully none of them had been serious. Yet. He'd been doing horrendously long hours and Charlie had been right to start looking for another surgeon to share the load. Those long days had been an excuse to avoid going home and facing the truth that Celine was never coming back. He'd worked until he was so tired he could fall into bed and sleep.

He should be grateful to Sarah. She hadn't forced this holiday on him, he had. By all accounts, she appeared to be the perfect locum, despite being an arrogant 'suit' from Auckland. Okay, not totally arrogant, but she was going to have difficulty fitting in here with those city manner-isms.

His eyes were riveted on the way her legs moved as she negotiated the crowd. Long, long legs that he imag-ined going— *Get a grip*. She was a colleague, not some female to be drooled over as though he was a sex-starved teenager. He winced. He was sex-starved. And only now beginning to notice. It had been so long he could barely remember what making love was like.

Now was not the time to find out. Which was another reason to wish Sarah on the other side of the planet.

Reaching her, he leaned down for her case at the same moment that she grabbed the handle.

'Let me,' he said quietly. And tried to breathe normally. The skin on the back on her hand was soft, smooth. Strands of blonde hair settled on her cheek. His heart stuttered. Such a mundane and delightful thing.

'I can manage,' she retorted.

'I know, but let me.'

Her mouth fashioned a fleeting smile. 'Thank you.'

This close he could see the dark shadows staining her upper cheeks. 'Do you feel up to driving, or would you rather come back for your car in the morning?'

'What, and have you hauling all those cases between

vehicles?' She managed another almost-smile. 'I'll follow you. Is it far?'

'About five kilometres, on the other side of town.' Thinking of the short street of shops, mostly farming and fishing suppliers, he knew Sarah would be shocked. There was one, surprisingly good, café run by a couple who'd opted for the quiet life after many years of running a business in Christchurch. Hopefully their coffee would be up to this woman's expectations.

Sarah pulled the outside door open. 'Allow me.'

'Oh, no. After you.' Dan gripped the edge of the door above her head.

She shrugged and ducked under his arm, out the doorway, bang into a throng of people crowding the steps. Leah danced along behind her. Fishermen crowded the porch, gathering to celebrate the rescue operation's success.

'Careful, lady!' someone exclaimed. 'Those steps are slippery.'

Sarah teetered at the edge of the top step. She put a hand out for balance but there was no railing to grab. Tripping, she made a desperate attempt to regain her footing. The heel of her sandal twisted, tipped her sideways and she went down hard, crying out as she thumped onto the concrete.

'Sarah.' Dan dropped her case, pushed through the men to crouch down beside her. 'Don't move. Let me look.'

She was on her backside, one leg twisted under her. 'I'm fine. Just help me up, please.' She put a hand out to him.

'Wait until I've checked your leg.'

'There's nothing wrong with it. It's my foot that hurts. Probably bruised.' Putting her hands down on either side of her hips, she tried to stand, but couldn't. 'Are you going to give me a hand, or do I ask someone else?'

'Sit still.' Those sandals weren't helping. 'How do you

expect to be able to stand up on that narrow spike you call a heel?'

'Typical male. Women are born to walk on heels,' she retorted through clenched teeth. Leaning to one side, she straightened her leg out from under her bottom, and bit down on her lip.

He gently felt her ankle, then her foot. The tissue was soft, already swelling, and her sharp intake of breath confirmed his suspicions. 'I think you've broken at least one bone. An X-ray will verify that.'

He'd call the radiology technician on the way to A and E. Technically a fracture in the foot could wait until the morning, but he didn't want this particular patient finding their small hospital lacking.

'That easily? That's crazy.' Sarah shook her head at her foot as though it was responsible for her predicament, and not those ridiculous shoes.

So much for Sarah taking over his practice this week. He should be pleased he'd be going to work. But even he understood his promise to Leah was meant to be kept. It didn't matter he was terrified he wouldn't measure up as a full-time dad for three months, and that Leah might revert to the disconsolate little girl he'd finally handed over to his family to help. He'd promised to try. Now, before he'd even started, their time together had to be postponed. He might've resented Sarah coming here, but right now he'd give anything to have her back on both feet and eager to get started.

CHAPTER THREE

SARAH hobbled after Dan as he carried a sleepy bundle of arms and legs into the weatherboard house. Leah had been tucked up in Jill's bed when Dan had finally had time to pick up his little girl on the way home from hospital.

Guilt for keeping this tot out late swamped Sarah. Due to her clumsiness Leah hadn't been with her dad when she should've been.

'Make yourself comfortable while I tuck Leah into bed,' Dan snapped over his shoulder, not easing Sarah's heavy heart.

He had every right to be annoyed with her. As had the other people whose time she'd intruded upon. Jill had driven her car here and someone had followed to pick her up. The radiology technician had gone into the hospital especially for her. And then there was Dan, who hadn't bothered to hide how he felt about this development.

Injuring her foot was a pain in the butt for her, too. If she hadn't been so intent on putting some space between her and Dan, it wouldn't have happened. The X-ray showed two broken bones. Her foot was twice its normal size and hurt like crazy. Thank goodness for painkillers.

Ignoring his order, Sarah followed Dan down the hall. Was he a good dad? Inexplicably she wanted to watch him tuck the child into bed, wanted another peep of Leah looking so cute with a blanket hitched under her chin and a bedraggled teddy bear squashed against her face. 'She's gorgeous,' she whispered, afraid of waking the girl, worried Dan might tell her to go away.

'Especially when she's asleep.' Dan's soft smile made Sarah's heart lurch. His big hand smoothed dark curls away from Leah's forehead. 'Actually, she's gorgeous all the time but, then, I'm biased.'

'So you should be.'

Dan placed feather-light kisses on his daughter's cheeks and forehead. 'Goodnight, sweetheart.'

From deep inside, in the place she hid unwanted emotions, something tugged at Sarah. A reminder of how much she'd been looking forward to having a family of her own when she and Oliver were married. That man had taken a lot from her.

'Are you all right?' Dan stood in front of her.

'Yes, of course.' Or could these emotions come from something else? An image of her own father tucking her into bed floated across her mind. As if. That was a fantasy. Dad had always been at work at her bedtime. No, she was overtired and getting confused.

'Your room is at the end of the hall. You've got an en suite bathroom so you won't have plastic toys to trip over.' Dan turned back towards the kitchen. 'I'll bring your cases in.'

'Thank you. I'll put the kettle on. Do you want a hot drink?'

'If you wait a few minutes, I'll get that. Go and put your foot up.'

'Dan, I am not incapable of boiling water.'

Loud knocking prevented Dan from answering, which by the tightening of his mouth and the narrowing of his eyes had saved her a blasting. Sarah trudged after him, her gait awkward because of the clunky moonboot clipped around her injured foot.

Dan growled at the visitor, 'Charlie, come in. I take it you've heard the news.'

'Three times since I got home from the river.' A dapper man in his sixties stepped into the kitchen. 'How is Dr Livingston?'

'I'm fine.' Sarah made it through the kitchen door and went towards the visitor with her hand out. 'Sarah Livingston.'

'Charlie Drummond. I'm sorry about your accident, lass.' Warmth emanated from his twinkling eyes.

She shrugged. 'Bit of a nuisance but nothing I can't deal with.'

'It changes everything.' Dan frowned. 'I've already told the nanny I'll need her for at least a week.'

Charlie shook his head. 'Oh, no, you don't. You're on leave. That's non-negotiable.'

'For goodness' sake, Charlie. There is no one else.' Dan's voice rose a few decibels. 'Until Sarah's back on her feet I'm your surgeon.'

'I'll ring around, see who I can find. Might don some scrubs myself.'

'It took months to find Sarah. You haven't got a chance in Hades of finding someone quickly, if at all.'

Sarah winced. 'Excuse me, but there's nothing wrong with my hearing.' She'd made a mess of things so she'd sort it. 'Or my brain. I'll be at work tomorrow.'

'Don't be ridiculous,' Dan snapped.

No one talked to her like that. 'Maybe late in the morning but I will be there. Trust me.' Sarah braced as a glare sliced at her, but when Dan said nothing she turned to the other man. 'I'm really sorry this has happened but it won't affect the board's plans too much.'

'Sarah, get real.' Dan dragged a hand through his damp

hair, making the thick curls stand up. Cute. Mouthwatering. Totally out of bounds.

Parking her bottom against the edge of the table, Sarah repeated, 'I'll be at work tomorrow.' She had to take control of the situation before Dan took over completely. 'Is there any surgery scheduled?'

Charlie smiled. 'It's a public holiday, remember? You've got a light week, emergencies not withstanding.'

'I'd planned on taking you in to meet any staff on duty, check out the theatre, and go over patient notes.' Dan shook his head in despair.

'Then there's no problem. We'll decide how to deal with emergencies if and when they arise.' Dan would be the last person she'd call for help. Having caused him enough trouble already, she was unusually contrite. 'If I have to, I can operate sitting down. It won't be easy but it's possible. Let's leave tomorrow's plans as they stand.'

And she could spend the night hoping she'd be fighting fit in the morning.

There was a speculative look in Dan's eyes as he regarded her, his arms folded over his thought-diverting chest.

'What?' How would it feel to curl up with him, her head lying against that chest? Protected and comforted? Huh! The last thing Dan Reilly was was comforting.

He shrugged. 'We'll see.'

'Sarah, I appreciate you coming down here at such short notice. I'm sure we can make this work until you're fully recovered,' Charlie said.

Dan grunted.

Sarah gripped the edge of the table tight as she sucked back a sharp retort. No need to aggravate Dan more than she already had. But hell if it wasn't tempting.

* * *

Dan was dog-tired. Every muscle ached. His head throbbed. He'd performed urgent surgery for a punctured lung following a car-versus-tree accident at three that morning. When he'd crawled into bed afterwards Leah had been grizzly so he'd had a squirming child to keep him awake for the remainder of the night. Then the nanny had been grumpy when he'd woken her for breakfast. Throw in a near-drowning, Sarah's arrival and accident, and he was almost comatose.

He peeped in on Leah. Lucky kid, dead to the world, unaware of the drama that had been going on and how it would affect the holiday he'd promised her.

Sarah's assumption that she'd be able to take over tomorrow wouldn't work, but he was fed up with arguing. Women. When they were in the mood they knew how to be difficult. It came naturally, like curves and bumps.

He sucked a breath. What was happening to him? He didn't usually give women more than cursory glances. Truth, with most of them he wouldn't even notice that they were female. But Sarah had woken him up in a hurry. He didn't know how. He just knew she had. Why her, of all people? Because she was one damned desirable lady.

She was one pain in the neck.

They were opposites: syrup and vinegar.

Opposites attracted.

He shouldn't be thinking about her except in her professional role. Not possible when they were going to be sharing such close living quarters. So how was a man to cope? How could he ignore what was right in front of him? Even with one foot strapped in that ugly moon boot she was more distracting than was good for him.

'Daddy?' Leah murmured in her sleep.

Gorgeous, that's what Sarah had called his little girl, and she was right. Beautiful, innocent, and in need of a mother figure. Someone special she could call hers; not all the aunts and cousins who were there for her. Someone to call Mummy. Someone he wasn't ready to bring into their lives.

'Go back to sleep, little one.' He tucked the blanket over her tiny shoulder. When she was like this he believed himself capable of being a good dad. It was the bad times when she hurt or cried that undermined his confidence. He loved how Leah trusted and loved him without question. He certainly didn't deserve it. Not when she spent most of her time in day care or with various other people while he ran around being busy and avoiding the issues that threatened to swamp him.

'You're so beautiful, my girl. Just like your mother. She'd be proud of you just for being so special and funny and adorable.' *But would Celine be pleased with the way her sister and mine are bringing you up for me? More like she'd be disappointed in the way I've ducked for cover every time the going's got tough.* He kissed Leah's soft cheek, his throat tightening at the feel of her soft skin. 'I love you.'

He stood gazing down at his child, the most important person in the world, and his heart swelled to the point it hurt. He mightn't have done much of a job of it yet but being a dad was so different from anything else he'd ever tried. Now he had to work hard to make up for lost time, learn to be there for Leah all the time. Where to start? What to do? Ask Bea and Jill. They wouldn't hold back in telling him, or coming to his rescue. He shuddered. No, it was time to stand on his own two feet.

Back in the lounge he dropped into a large armchair and studied the other female in his house. The enigmatic one. The more he saw of Sarah, the more she piqued his curiosity. Why had she been available to come here at such short notice? He'd read her CV, knew she held a partnership in some fancy, private surgical hospital with her father and some other dude. So why'd she been available?

'Does Leah sleep right through the night?' Sarah spoke in her lilting voice, now tinged with exhaustion.

'Like a log.' Usually. When she wasn't crying for Mummy. Which happened less and less these days, he realised with a start.

Sarah didn't have children and her résumé hadn't mentioned a husband. Why, considering she was thirty-five? Divorced? What if she hated kids? His heart thumped. He wouldn't accept that. 'Are you used to being around children?'

'Not a lot.'

'Got any nieces or nephews?' This wasn't looking good. How would she cope with Leah?

'No.'

'Siblings?'

'My brother died when he was eighteen. I was sixteen at the time.' Her voice was flat, but there was pain in her eyes, in her fists on her knees.

Her words sent shivers down his spine, made him gasp. 'Sarah, I'm truly sorry. I can be too nosey at times.' There'd been a stoplight in her eyes, but he'd pressed on with his questions regardless, too concerned about his own problems.

What to say now? A tragedy like that stayed with a person for ever. What had happened to her brother? Was there more to her story? For sure he wasn't about to ask. Not with that massive chunk of hurt radiating out from those eyes. But he understood firsthand how death changed things. Everything crashed to a halt. You didn't even notice life was still going on around you. Only after months of agony did you slowly begin to move again, begin to function semi-normally. It took even longer to recover from the guilt. 'How awful.' How inadequate.

She jerked her head affirmatively. 'It certainly is.'

Is. Not was. Hadn't she got over it a tiny bit? Her fingers were twisted and interlaced in her lap, her eyes downcast. Dan fought the impulse to reach for her, hold her safe. A friendly gesture that she definitely wouldn't appreciate. When she finally raised her head he saw sadness and loneliness lurking in those compelling eyes.

Then he surprised himself. 'Leah was two when her mother died.' Which was too much information. He didn't want to share personal details with Sarah, not even one. It was enough that they were sharing his practice, and his home.

Celine slipped into his mind again. For the past two years he'd taken the approach of ignoring the gaping hole left by her passing, hoping that one day he'd find it filled in with life's trivia. In reality he should've been facing up to things, like looking after his daughter instead of leaving that to everyone else. Like accepting he couldn't wind back the clock and pack Celine up to take her home to the city she'd loved and missed. Back to her interfering mother who'd put those ideas of distrust in Celine's head.

'That's really tough. For both of you.' Sarah's tone was compassionate. 'How does Leah cope?'

'She's very resilient.' More so than him. 'Most of the time. She has her moments. We manage.' Sort of. With a lot of help. 'I hope you'll get on with her.'

'I doubt I'll see much of her.' Then she changed the subject. 'Tell me how your local health board operates. It seems to be very successful when others in remote areas have failed.'

'It wasn't always like this but with a bit of lateral thinking the board members came up with a scheme to employ a full-time surgeon. Instead of sending patients out of the area, they contracted for the overflow from Christchurch public hospitals. It was a perfect solution for my wife and me as we wanted to be near my family once Leah was born.' Yes, *we* wanted to make the move. Celine had been as much for it as he had. She'd loved her horses; enjoyed getting to know Jill, the sister she hadn't grown up with. When had he forgotten that? Had he been so immersed in self-pity that he hadn't looked at all sides of the problem? Celine had had a part to play in her welfare too. Because the other side of the story was that he fitted in here, loved giving back to his community through his work.

'So you grew up in Port Weston?' An alien female voice intruded.

He blinked. Sarah sat opposite him, an expression of polite interest on her beautiful face. 'Yes, I did.' What had they been talking about? Of course, the hospital. What else? That's all Sarah would be interested in. 'There's been a flow-on effect for the town from having the surgical unit here. Most patients coming for elective surgery bring friends or relatives with them. Those people need entertaining, feeding, housing.'

'So you've got a lively metropolis out there somewhere?' Her sweet, tired smile pulled at his heart.

How could that be when he'd known her less than twelve hours? Something to think about—later.

Back to her question. 'Not quite what you're used to.' The understatement of the year. 'But the shops are improving, and you'll be glad to know our café is first rate.'

'Can't go past a great coffee shop.'

He saw her stifled yawn in her tightened mouth and clenched jaw, and leapt up. 'Here I am blathering on and you're half-asleep. I'll help you get ready for bed.' And gain some freedom from those all-seeing eyes.

Taking her elbow, he helped her up onto her good foot, then without warning swung her into his arms and carried her down to her room. She felt wonderful. Soft. Warm. Desirable.

He croaked, 'Stop wriggling. You're making it difficult for me to hold you.' *And causing certain soft feminine parts of your anatomy to rub against my chest. Very nice.* Shocked described how he felt. And hot. Hard. Stunned.

'Then put me down,' she responded, instantly tense and remaining that way until he sat her on the bed and bent down to remove the moon boot.

'I'll do that.' She yanked her leg away from him, groaning when pain jagged her.

'Let's be reasonable about this. You're all-out tired and with my help you'll be in bed a lot quicker. Probably with much less pain. I am a doctor, remember?' Great logic that.

'I'm sure you're right, but I'll manage,' she wheezed through gritted teeth. 'I have to get used to this boot as soon as possible.'

So she was concerned she wouldn't be functioning properly tomorrow.

'Take it easy and leave worrying about how you're going to get around till the morning.' He stared at the three cases he'd hauled in earlier. Gucci, of course. 'Which bag has your night things?'

Sarah took the negligee he finally found and pointed to the door. 'I'll do this.'

Plastering his best bedside manner on his face, he put a hand under her arm and, trying to ignore his increasing pulse, said, 'There's the easy way, and the hard way. Let's go for easy.'

She tipped her head back to stare up at him and he saw the exhaustion in her eyes, in her loose shoulders, in the slack hands lying in her lap.

'You're right.' And then she lifted her top up over her head.

Dan's mouth dried, and it was a lifetime before he moved to help her. Her creamy skin was like warm satin. The swell of her breasts in their frothy, black lace cups caused him to bite painfully into his bottom lip. His hands shook when he took the garment from her and tossed it onto a chair in the corner. It missed.

Her fingers fumbled at the button on her waistband. He tried to help but she pushed his hands away. Lifting his eyes to her face, he saw the faint pink colour rising in her cheeks. Had he embarrassed her with his quickening interest? *Daniel Reilly, you need your head read. You have to live with this woman for twelve whole weeks. Keep everything above board.*

'Here, I'll lift you so you can slide your trousers down,' he muttered, and placing his hands on her elbows focused on being practical. As if. But he tried.

Next he knelt to remove the moon boot, taking care not to jar her foot. Under his fingers her satin skin reminded him of sultry summer nights. He ached to caress it. Common sense prevailed. Just.

'Thanks.' Sarah flopped back against the pillow, pulling the covers over herself. Then she closed her eyes. The determination and fierce independence she'd displayed all evening disappeared, leaving her looking defenceless. Any pain from her foot was hidden behind her eyelids.

Without thinking, he reached out to brush a strand of hair off her cheek, hesitated, withdrew. How would he explain such impulsiveness? She was one tough lady, and he suspected that sassy attitude hid a lot of things from the world. Things he'd like to learn more about. But right now it was way past time to get out of her room. 'See you in the morning.'

He'd made her door when he heard her whisper. 'Is it safe to open a window? It's very stuffy in here.'

'That's because we're between rain spells again.' He crossed to the windows. 'And of course it's safe. You're not in the city now.'

'I suppose you leave your doors unlocked.' She rolled onto her side and the covers slid off her shoulders.

Again Dan's gaze was drawn to her flawless skin and her negligee highlighting the swell of her breasts. He mightn't have had a sex life for a very long time but suddenly that didn't seem to mean a thing. It was as though he'd—she'd—flicked a switch and, whammo!

'Just one window open?' he said breathlessly, his throat as tight as a clamped artery.

'I think so. Is that the surf I can hear?'

'Yes. We're quite close to the sea.' He made for the door again, this time with no intention of stopping, regardless of what she said. *Keep talking so she can't get a word in.* 'The high fence surrounding the property is to stop Leah from wandering down to the water. Even with the main road and a stretch of grassed land between us, I don't take any chances.'

Of course he wouldn't. That much Sarah had figured out already. A yawn stretched her mouth. Despite the exhaustion gripping her, she doubted she was about to get much sleep. If the pain didn't keep her awake then a load of other concerns would. For starters, she'd let Dan down big time. He needed her here, whether he accepted it or not.

Already she sensed her time in Port Weston wasn't just about sorting out her own life. She may have come to free up Dan's life, but now she wanted to do more for him. And for his daughter. But what? Her experience of children and happy families was non-existent.

An image of a darling little girl floated across her mind. Leah. How to remain aloof when the child had already touched her heart? She had to. That's all there was to it. Getting attached to Dan's daughter had no place in her life. And she must not listen to the increasingly loud ticking of her biological clock.

What about Dan himself? His wife had died. No wonder he was running solo here with Leah. It wouldn't be easy to put his loss behind him with a child to care for.

So she had to get a grip on her unprecedented attraction to him. But what would his kisses be like? Hungry? Soft? Demanding? *Hello, Sarah, back to earth, please.*

The man crashing through her head placed a glass by her bed. 'Thought you might like some water.'

'Thanks.' She clenched her fists. How long had he been standing there? 'I don't usually make such a hash of things. I'm truly sorry.' But she felt even more regretful she wouldn't taste his kisses. Kisses had to be avoided if she was to keep her relationship with Dan strictly professional.

'It was an accident, okay?'

'You're not putting off doing all those dad things Leah's hankering for.' She pulled the bedcover back up to her neck. He could stop peeking at her negligee. He'd already had more than an eyeful. Admittedly she'd enjoyed the appreciative glint in his eyes. Enjoyed? Get real. When he looked at her so intently she became a very desirable woman. What a salve for her battered self-esteem. By having an affair, Oliver had made her feel unwanted, undesirable.

Dan hesitated, his hand on the light switch. 'Why don't

you wear oversized T-shirts to bed, like most women I know?'

'They didn't have any in my colour.'

How many women did he see in their night attire?

CHAPTER FOUR

'HURRY up, Daddy. We'll be late,' Leah shrieked the next morning, bouncing between Dan's knees as he brushed her hair.

'Stand still, young lady,' Dan answered at a much lower decibel, his eyes narrowed as he fought the hair into submission.

'Flicker's waiting for me.' Leah bit into her bottom lip as she struggled to keep from jiggling.

Sarah grinned at Dan. 'You need to speed up, man.'

'I'm never fast enough for Leah. She was born in a hurry.'

'Flicker doesn't go very fast. Auntie Bea won't let him cos I could fall off.' Leah twisted around to stare at her father. 'You're riding Jumbo.'

'I was afraid of that.' Dan smiled at his daughter, love shining out of his eyes. 'Of course, if you don't stand quietly while I do these ponytails, neither of us will be riding any horse today.'

'Daddy, we must. Flicker will miss me.'

'Is Flicker your horse?' Sarah asked the little girl.

Big blue eyes peeped back at her from under an overlong fringe. 'He's Auntie Bea's but I'm the only person allowed to ride him. Can you ride a horse?'

'Me? No way. I don't like being so far off the ground.'
Anything higher than a short stool was too high.

Dan wrapped an elastic tie around a ponytail, his gaze
firmly on the wayward curls he was struggling to contain.
The part between the ponytails was well to the side of the
middle of Leah's head. 'Have you ever tried?'

'Once, when I was about Leah's age. The horse took
exception to having me on its back and tossed me off. No
amount of bribery got me back on.'

'I haven't been throwed off.' Leah's eyes glowed with
pride.

Dan put the brush down and reached for the ribbons
lying on the table. 'Nearly there, missy. Flicker will think
you're looking cool today.' His mouth curved with a smile
just for his daughter. Pride and love mingled across his
face, his big hands gentle as he tried to fashion the blue
ribbons into bows.

Leah stood absolutely still for the first time, her elbows resting on Dan's thighs, her little freckle-covered
face puckered up in thought.

Sarah caught her breath. They belonged together. Father
and daughter. If only she had a camera to take a picture
showing the love between these two. The air was warm
with it. There was a vulnerability in Dan's eyes she'd never
expected from the gruff man she'd known so far.

Her stomach tightened. What these two had was special, something she'd like to share. What? She wanted to
be with Dan and his daughter? Only for the time she was
in Port Weston, of course. Of course. Because she still
loved Oliver, hard as that was to admit after everything
he'd done to her.

'Sarah, do I look pretty?' Leah bounced in front of her,
unwittingly dragging Sarah's attention onto her and away
from the desperate thoughts that threatened to ruin her

day. Leah had pulled away from Dan's hands, effectively ruining the bow he was working on.

'Very pretty. Now, hand me those bows and I'll help your dad make you even prettier.' Her throat closed over as she quickly tied two big bows, trying hard not to feel as though she was missing out on something very important. She reached over and flicked one of the ponytails, making Leah giggle. 'If he hasn't already, then Flicker's going to fall in love with you.'

Who wouldn't fall in love with the child? Panic seized Sarah. What if she did? She mustn't. There were too many complications for all of them otherwise. And the child must be protected first and foremost.

Dan shook his head in disgust. 'That easy, huh?' He stood and stretched. 'If you're not careful, the job's yours while you're here.'

She might get to like that. 'Guess you've never had long hair.'

'You think I should've put my hair in ponytails? What sort of guys did you mix with as a teenager?' He blinked at her, but she obviously wasn't meant to answer. 'We'd better get going before my sister sends out a search party.' He ran his knuckles over his bristly chin, worry clouding his eyes. 'I hope I survive the morning.'

'You can't keep up with Leah?' Sarah challenged with a laugh, trying to lift his spirits.

'Sometimes I wonder if she's really only four, she's so confident.'

'Four to your, what? Thirty-two,-three?'

'Flattery is supposed to get you everything. Try thirty-five.' His lips widened from tight to relaxed.

The same age as her. 'Where'd you go to med school?' They'd have been training around the same time.

'Dunedin, then Christchurch to specialise. You?'

'Auckland and London.' Where she'd met Oliver. At first they'd been friends. Liar. She'd thought he was hot from the moment she'd set eyes on him, and he'd known it. But she'd finished her specialist training before succumbing to his charm and going out with him.

'Daddy, come on.' Leah grabbed his hand and began tugging him towards the back door.

'Sure you'll be all right? Nothing you need, like a sandwich, another cup of tea?' Reluctance shadowed his voice. Was it the horse riding he worried he couldn't cope with? Or Leah? 'You could come with us.'

'I don't think so. I don't know much about entertaining children.'

'Sure you don't want to start this morning?'

'Stop procrastinating. Apart from getting a sore backside, you'll be fine. Look how excited Leah is about this.'

'Yeah, that's the problem. And the fact I've forgotten which end of a horse is which.'

'You're not expected to be an expert. Dan, go, now.' Sarah deliberately stood up and turned her back on him, reaching for the kettle to show she could manage. She didn't turn around until the door closed quietly behind her.

Then she stared out the window, watching Dan's vehicle bouncing down the drive, rolling along the highway until it disappeared out of sight around a bend. The tightness in her shoulders eased. This was the first time she'd been alone, without Dan in reach, since she'd charged down the beach yesterday. She should be pleased not to have his disturbing eyes watching her, his acerbic tongue ready to refute everything she said.

Instead loneliness threatened to swamp her. In Auckland she never felt lonely, despite not having a wide circle of friends. There were shops or the hospital to keep her occupied. Here—here there wasn't a lot in the way of distractions now that Dan had gone out.

Beyond the road the sea kept rolling onto the shore. Wind whipped spume off the hypnotic wave-tops. A long, wild coastline with no one in sight. 'What a godforsaken place.' She kept staring at it until a kind of peace stole over her. 'But it's sort of beautiful.'

The strident tones of the phone awoke Sarah from a deep sleep. Confused, she stared around at the unfamiliar room. Her vision filled with soft, warm colours: blues, a dash of yellow, a hint of green. A complete contrast to the clean, white walls and terracotta furnishings of her Auckland apartment. Then she remembered. Port Weston. Bad-tempered Dr Reilly. Her broken bones.

Pushing off the couch, she hopped to the table where she'd unwisely left the phone. Her moon boot bumped against a chair. Pain snatched her breath away. Gripping the back of the chair, she fumbled with the phone, anxious not to miss the call and give Dan another reason to believe she was incompetent.

'Hello, Dr Reilly's residence.'

'This is the hospital A and E department. Is Dan there?'

Apprehension made Sarah straighten up. Please, not an emergency. 'Dan's gone horse riding at his sister's.'

'No wonder I can't reach him on his cellphone.' The caller sounded harassed. 'No coverage up there.'

'Can I do anything? I'm Sarah Livingston, a doctor.'

'Thank goodness.' The relief was obvious. 'I'm Alison Fulton, A and E specialist. We've got a six-year-old girl with appendicitis and, if I'm not mistaken, we need to hurry. Apparently the child's been complaining of stomach pains for hours.'

'I'll come straight away.' This wouldn't be so bad. She'd be able to handle an appendectomy sitting down.

'Thank you so much.'

'You're aware I can't drive at the moment?' Sarah knew how well hospital grapevines worked.

'Dan mentioned it. I'll get someone to pick you up.' Then the specialist's voice changed, became concerned. 'You do feel up to this? I don't want you to think you have to come in. I haven't tried Charlie's phone yet. He's my last resort, though I know he's gone after another trout.'

So Dan had been warning people about her situation. Looking out for her? Or indicating he'd prefer he was called in so he had an excuse to return to work? Putting all the confidence she could muster into her voice, Sarah reassured Alison. 'Operating will be fine. Just send that car.'

She crossed her fingers. Just the one op, please.

Wee Emma Duncan's face was contorted with a mix of fear and pain as she lay on the bed, tucked into her father's side. Her eyes were enormous in her pale face. Neither of her parents looked much better.

'Emma, I'm Dr Sarah, and I'm going to make your tummy better.' Sarah winked at the frightened girl. Then she introduced herself to the parents, trying to ignore their obvious glances at her crutches. 'Mr and Mrs Duncan, Theatre's ready so we'll be getting started very shortly.'

'Where's Dan?' Emma's father asked.

'I'm his replacement while he's on leave.' Sarah forced a smile at their obvious distrust of a stranger. 'Please don't be worried about the fact that I've broken a couple of bones in my foot. I assure you my operating skills are still intact.'

'It's just we know Dan,' Mr Duncan explained.

Not used to being questioned about her role, Sarah tried

to imagine what these parents must be going through. They'd be terrified for their beautiful girl. 'I do understand, but the real concern's whether I'm good at what I do. Dan and Charlie must believe I am, or they wouldn't have taken me on.'

'Never mind the fact that there wasn't a queue of applicants for the job,' Sarah muttered to herself. That wasn't the point. She was a good surgeon.

Emma's mother gazed at her daughter with such love Sarah's heart expanded. To be a parent had to be one of the most wondrous privileges on earth. For the second time that day deep regret at her childlessness gripped Sarah. Within twenty-four hours Port Weston had got to her in ways she'd never have expected. Or was it Dr Dan sneaking in under her skin that had her emotions rocking all over the place? Because something sure was.

Back to Emma. 'Do you want to tell me how long you've had this tummyache?' Sarah asked.

'Em started complaining first thing this morning, Doctor.' Her father still looked uncertain but thankfully he answered all Sarah's questions thoroughly and quickly.

Sarah read the lab results and Alison Fulton's notes. Emma's high white-cell count backed the diagnosis of appendicitis. But it worried Sarah that there were indications of a burst appendix.

An orderly appeared at the doorway. 'Hey, Emma. How's my favourite niece? I'm going to take you for a short ride on the bed.'

Was everyone related in this town? How weird was that? Sarah's living relatives numbered two, her mother and father. She couldn't begin to imagine what it would be like to have cousins, uncles, grandparents, all those extra people in her life. Certainly had no idea how different growing up might have been. If she ever fell in love again, maybe she should find a man with relatives she could come to know and love. Her ex had only one sister who lived in London and they weren't close.

Sarah spoke to Emma's mother. 'It's Gayle, isn't it?'

The woman nodded. 'Sorry if we seem silly but—'

'It's okay. I know I'm asking the impossible but please try not to worry too much. I'll come and see you the moment I've finished,' Sarah tried to reassure her.

Then a nurse helped Sarah to scrub up. Surrounded by people she didn't know, about to operate at a hospital she'd never worked in before, it all seemed a little surreal. But theatres were theatres wherever she went. Nurses and anaesthetists did the same job everywhere. She just had to get over herself and concentrate on Emma's operation.

Jill popped her head around the corner. 'Heard you got called in and thought you might like a friendly face.'

'Yes, definitely.' Warmth washed through Sarah as she raised a thumb in acknowledgment, thrilled that Jill had been so considerate.

'We've found you a stool if you need it,' Jill told her.

In Theatre Hamish, the anaesthetist Sarah had met moments earlier, administered the drug that would keep Emma unconscious throughout the operation.

Sarah shuffled awkwardly on her injured foot, trying to find the most comfortable position without having to use the stool. Taking a deep breath, she lifted a scalpel and looked around at the attending staff. 'Ready?'

She concentrated on finding the infected appendix and assessing the situation. 'We're in luck. It hasn't perforated.'

Jill held out a clamp in a gloved hand. 'Poor kid. She still must've been hurting bad.'

Sarah clamped off all circulation to the appendix. 'Wonder what took her family so long to bring her in?'

'They live about a hundred and fifty kilometres from

here, up a valley in very difficult terrain,' Jill explained. 'It's no easy ride out of those hills.'

Sarah moved abruptly to one side to get a better view of the incision. Pain shot through her foot, diverting her attention briefly.

'You okay?' Hamish was watching her closely. 'Use the stool.'

'Thanks, but I prefer standing.' The stool might be too clumsy. Hamish's concern for her was nice. So far, working with this team was going well: no tension, everyone confident in their role yet also believing in each other's competence. Very different from the surgical hospital back home where everyone seemed to be trying to outdo each other on a regular basis. Today, here, she was beginning to understand how jaded she'd become and that her father might've been right to nudge her out of town. Working in this theatre was like a breath of fresh air.

Finally Sarah began tying off internally. The appendix stump. The blood vessels she'd had to cut. Her hands were heavy, like bricks. More thread required. Her back ached from the lopsided stance she'd maintained to counterbalance her boot-encased foot.

There was a soft whooshing sound as the door swung open, then closed. Sarah didn't have to be told Dan had arrived. With every nerve ending in her body she sensed his presence. She tried to concentrate on her work and not glance up, but her eyes lifted anyway. She looked directly at him. Warmth spread through her tired muscles and momentarily she felt recharged and capable of going on for ever.

He was fully scrubbed up, looking at Emma carefully. Checking up on his replacement? Sarah tried to read his eyes, saw a reprimand.

'Want a hand?' His voice was muffled behind his mask,

but there was no mistaking his anger. What exactly had she done wrong?

'I'm perfectly capable of finishing off.' She didn't need his help. Except that moments ago she'd noted how tired she'd become. Emma was her priority, not her pride. 'Could you close up for me?' she asked quietly.

Admiration filtered through his eyes, toning down the anger. Relief relaxed Sarah. She'd done the right thing. Gingerly shuffling sideways, she made room for Dan. Despite his unnecessary disapproval, it felt so right standing beside him here in Theatre, two professionals working to help Emma.

'Alison's message came through as we got to the bottom of the valley so I dropped Leah off at her nanny's and came straight over in case I was required. Obviously I wasn't.' Dan deftly pressed the suture needle through the flesh to pull another section of the wound together. 'You still should've got someone in to assist you, under the circumstances.'

'I'm glad it wasn't anything difficult,' Sarah admitted. But when Dan raised one eyebrow at her in an 'I told you so' fashion she retorted, 'There wasn't anyone else. Alison checked, and she was too busy to help.'

'I can see Emma was in excellent hands.' The grudging admittance in his voice confused her. Why did he find it hard to accept she knew what she was doing?

As Sarah swabbed away a speck of blood Jill reached across from the other side of the operating table to do it. Lifting her gaze to meet the other woman's, Sarah nearly choked. Jill was winking at her, her eyes holding a knowing glint. It could be interpreted in a trillion ways, but Sarah bet Jill still had ideas of matchmaking. A scheme that was doomed to crash and burn. Sarah had to go back to Auckland, if not at the end of her contract then some time in the next six months. Her father didn't mean for her to walk away from her partnership, just recoup her energy. Neither did she want to. She liked her comfortable lifestyle and the predictability of her job in Auckland.

Get real. You were bored. Exhausted. Fed up. Burying yourself in work to get over a broken heart. Why would you want to go back to that? Because it was the only life she knew and understood.

So, learn a new one. This is the perfect opportunity. A trickle of excitement seeped into her veins, lifted her spirits. Could she do that? Did she want to? She grinned. Possibly.

She headed for the scrub room, struggling to remove her gown. Her fingers fumbled with the knots on the ties.

'Let me do that.'

She hadn't heard Dan come in. 'Thanks.'

His fingers covered hers, took the cotton ties and tugged lightly to undo the impossible knots. 'You ready to go home?'

Home? 'Sure.'

Dan's fingers rested on the back of her neck. A simple touch, a very potent touch that made her feel good about herself. At the same time he disturbed her on a deeper level. Right now it was all too much to take in, she needed time to sift through the emotions pinging around her head.

She twisted around. 'I promised Emma's parents I'd see them as soon as I was finished.'

'No one expects you to. You must be exhausted.' His hand didn't shift.

'Maybe, but I do keep my word. And they must be fraught with worry by now.' With effort she shuffled away, forcing his arm to drop. She had no right to continue standing there enjoying his touch, no matter how innocently he gave it. She couldn't afford to surrender to wild needs. But, heaven knew, she wanted to. And, worse, it was hard to ignore those needs. But to give in to them with this man? After knowing him how long? One day. No, she must not. Hadn't she learnt anything from Oliver?

'You're right.' Daniel tugged his gown off. 'I'll come with you.'

All she was going to do was tell Emma's parents that their precious little girl was doing fine, but Dan accompanying her seemed right. Like they were a team. Scary. So she reacted with a verbal swipe. 'You're on holiday.'

'Coming from a large city, you can't be expected to appreciate how our patients are also our families, or our friends and neighbours. We treat the whole picture, not just the immediate illness.'

'I understand.' How mortifying that Dan thought so badly of her. He was totally wrong. She did care for her patients outside the operating theatre. *Huh? How often do you see any of your patients in any other capacity?* They come for consultation, surgery, a follow-up visit, then goodbye. She swallowed her chagrin. Dan had a point. But that didn't mean she wasn't as compassionate as he was. 'What are we waiting for?'

Jill poked her head around the door. 'Since you're both here, Anders and his father would love it if you dropped in on them when you're done with the Duncans.'

'Good idea.' The more time spent at the hospital meant less at home with only Dan and the conflicting emotions he stirred up. Sarah swung awkwardly on her crutches, hoping the ward wasn't too far away.

'Here, park your bottom in this.' Dan spun a wheelchair in her direction.

Great. 'I don't think so.' Where'd he found that so quickly?

'No one's going to think worse of you for conserving

your energy and protecting your foot.' Dan waited to push her. 'Sit,' he growled when she started to protest.

'Oh, all right.' Sarah eased into the wheelchair. Arguing took too much energy.

'Very gracious,' Dan muttered in her ear as he took the crutches from her.

Emma's parents were soon brought up to date and then a nurse took them to see their daughter. Dan whizzed Sarah along to the Starnes men, Jill going with them.

Anders and his father were sitting up in their respective beds, two dark heads turning at the sound of Sarah's chair wheels on the vinyl floor.

'Are you the doctors who saved me?' Anders raised his arm and winced.

'Don't move too much yet,' Dan advised in a friendly tone Sarah hadn't heard before. 'That shoulder will be tender for a while. This is Dr Livingston and I'm Dan Reilly.'

'We're very grateful for all you did for my boy,' the older man said, thrusting out his hand. 'Peter Starne.'

'You're both looking a lot better than the last time I saw you.' Sarah smiled as she took his hand.

'Unlike you, Doctor. What happened?'

'A slippery step got in my way.'

Dan's mood changed and he glared at the father. 'You're very fortunate, the pair of you. That's a wild coast out there.'

Peter looked sheepish. 'I know. I was an idiot to take Anders fishing off those rocks. Won't be doing that again in a hurry.'

'Glad you've learnt your lesson,' Dan snapped. 'A lot of people were involved in your rescue and any one of them could've been hurt. Or worse.'

Jill stepped closer, gripped Dan's elbow in warning. 'Pat

and Malcolm have been in to talk to Peter and Anders this morning. They've got the message loud and clear.'

'They'd…' Dan spluttered to a stop as Jill wrenched him away.

'Come on. You can show Sarah around the medical ward.' Out in the corridor Jill continued talking to Dan. 'Leave it. Pat gave them enough of a talking to about safety to last them a lifetime. They don't need the same lecture from you.'

'Why not? Did you see him? He looked embarrassed, not contrite.' Dan stared at Jill. 'He should be on his knees, thanking every last man who went out in that horrendous sea to save his butt.'

'Keep your voice down. This is a medical ward, not the sideline of a rugby field.' Jill cuffed him lightly. 'I understand how you feel, what with Malcolm being one of those men, but it's not our place to tell Peter Starne.'

Dan jerked a thumb over his shoulder. 'I haven't finished in there.'

Jill looked exasperated. 'Dan, leave it.'

'I need to check the boy's dislocated shoulder.'

Sarah looked up at Dan and asked gently, trying to keep reproof out of her voice so as not to antagonise him any more, 'Today's the first day of your holiday, remember? That means I'll take a look at Anders.'

He frowned. 'Don't you think you're being a little too keen to get off the mark, Doctor?'

'I suppose I could return to the house and put my foot up on pillows, demand pots of tea, and flick through magazines to while away the rest of the day.'

'What a good idea.' His frown lightened and he began pushing her. 'Let's go.'

'Dan.' Jill stepped in front of the wheelchair, effectively

stopping Dan's progress. Her eyes drilled into him. 'You're being obstructive'

'I'm trying to do the right thing for Sarah.' He began pushing the chair around Jill. 'Okay, she can go over next week's surgery schedule while I see to Anders.'

Sarah retorted, 'And then you will hand over the reins and go enjoy yourself.'

When the wheelchair moved off at speed she widened her smile. Men. Obstinate creatures.

'Why are women so difficult?' Dan asked Jill as he leaned against the nurses' station, reading Anders's case notes. 'Why aren't they more like men? What's wrong with accepting your limitations?'

Jill cocked her head on one side and looked at him, her earlier annoyance with him gone. 'You're talking about Sarah, I presume.'

Dan didn't like that all-knowing glimmer in his sister-in-law's eyes. 'Who else?'

'Sarah's being a real champ. She's certainly not bemoaning the fact she's been incapacitated, despite being in some pain. Nothing stopped her coming in when Alison called her for help.'

Dan's gaze rested on Sarah as she studied patient files at a desk at the other end of the ward. A little frown creased her brow as she concentrated. He'd noted that frown in Theatre when she'd focused on Emma, again when she'd explained everything about the operation to Gayle and John. He'd wanted to smooth the crease away then. He wanted to smooth it away now. What a distraction the woman was becoming. A very sexy distraction.

'Tell me.' Jill picked up the conversation again. 'What would you have done in the same circumstances? Stayed at home, grizzling? Or would you've got on with things, taking it on the chin like a man?'

'I am a man.'

'Yeah, and I don't think Sarah's a woman who spends a lot of time feeling sorry for herself.'

'You've got her all figured out already?'

'Call it woman's intuition, but I think our locum is one very self-contained lady who doesn't shirk her duties.'

'Huh,' Dan muttered. He had a sneaking suspicion Jill was right. 'That'll make Leah one happy kid. She's not sure of Sarah yet, gave her the fifth degree about her broken foot over breakfast.' Dan grinned. 'Then told Sarah she was naughty for going too fast and falling over. That child takes after her dad.'

Jill rolled her eyes. 'Poor little tyke.'

'Thanks very much. Glad to know who my friends are.' He covered a yawn. 'Having Sarah in the house might work out after all.' He'd get help with Leah and Sarah would learn to enjoy being around kids.

'Sleepless night?' Jill asked, her eyes widening and her mouth twitching.

'Sort of.' He'd taken hours to fall asleep, only to dream of creamy skin and a black lace bra filled to perfection. Not to mention a beautiful face and endearing smile. 'I think I'm already winding down into holiday mode.'

'Oh, sure. Nothing to do with your house guest, I presume.' Jill elbowed him. 'Go on, get out of here. It's time you had some fun. And I'm not just referring to Leah. Sarah could be the best thing to happen to you in a long time.'

It's time he had some sex, he knew that. But not with Dr Livingston. There again, why not? She was only here for a few months, long enough to have some fun with but not so long as to create problems. Like which side of the wardrobe she could hang her clothes. As if there'd ever be enough wardrobe space for all her outfits.

No, if he was getting back into the man-woman thing then it should be with a woman he could settle down and have more kids with. That job description did not suit Sarah. Except she'd been good with Leah that morning, and Gayle had said Sarah knew how to talk to Emma before her surgery.

On the other hand, she was too upmarket for Port Weston. For him. And he'd learned the hard way what happened when you tried to take the city out of a woman. It didn't work. She'd start blaming him for everything that went wrong, looking for problems that didn't exist.

In his pocket his phone vibrated as a text came through. He sighed as he read the message. Leah needed to change her top and Dan hadn't left the bag of clean clothes with the nanny.

One step forward, one back. Or was it sideways?

CHAPTER FIVE

'CAN we pull over for a moment?' Sarah asked Dan on the way to the hospital and her Saturday-morning patient round three days later.

'Something wrong?' He turned his four-wheel-drive into a lay-by on the ocean side of the road.

'Not at all.' As the vehicle stopped she pushed her door open and began to ease down on her feet, favouring the bad one. 'I want some wind and salt spray on my face.' The huge breakers that continuously rolled in fascinated her, drawing her into their rhythm. They lulled her to sleep at night, lifted her mood during the day. Very different from the sounds of downtown Auckland—dense traffic, sirens, people of every nationality calling out to each other.

'Can I sit in here, Daddy? I'm listening to the Singing Frogs.' Leah was belted into a back seat, twisting the cord of her small CD player.

'Sure can, kiddo.' Dan appeared at Sarah's side in double-quick time. 'This coastline is wild. Crazy and dangerous. It's very much a part of Coasters and who they are.'

'You're so right.' He could be referring to himself. Wild, crazy and dangerous. Definitely dangerous to her equilibrium. She breathed in the vibrant air, smelt salt and wet sand and seagulls. The thudding waves drowned out extraneous sounds except for the screeching gulls rising and falling on the air currents above them.

'Have you been to the Coast before?' Dan's hands rested on his slim hips, which drew her eye.

'Never.' She concentrated on the sea, trying to ignore the man. 'There weren't a lot of holidays when I was growing up, and none to the South Island.' Her brother, Bobby, might have got ill while they were away, which would have thrown her mother into a spin. 'And I confess that as an adult I've tended to head overseas for vacations. Not very patriotic of me, I guess, but the friends I used to go away with are more interested in the exotic and I've always gone along.' Even to her that sounded like a copout. 'Willingly,' she added.

Dan shook his head at her. 'Tourists say this is exotic. They pay to come here.'

'Tourists usually do pay.' Stop being difficult with him. 'You're right. I should've seen my own country by now. Maybe I'll have time to look around a bit while I'm here.' She could take a day trip on her day off. Shifting the conversation away from herself, she asked, 'Did I hear you've got a sister in Australia?'

'Pauline, our adopted sister. I'd like to take Leah over to get to know her extended family some time.'

'Adopted? Older or younger?' Family. Why did everything come back to that? Was she just being over-sensitive since Oliver had left her?

'She comes between Bea and me. Her mother and ours were sisters. Pauline's mother was a single mum and when she died in a house fire our parents naturally took Pauline in. No one ever knew who her father was.'

'What a wonderful thing for your parents to do.' Hers couldn't wait to see the back of each other after her brother had died. The stress and pressure of losing their son had taken a big toll. And no matter how hard she'd tried, she hadn't been able to make them understand she'd needed them to stay together as much as Bobby had.

Dan looked at her in disbelief. 'Not at all. That's what families are all about.'

Really? He didn't get how lucky he was. 'When did you last see Pauline?'

Dan turned to stare out over the waves. 'Two years ago. She came over for Celine's funeral and stayed on for two weeks, helping me get my head around what had happened. She was incredibly patient with me.'

'Had your wife been ill?' All these questions. Any minute he'd tell her to mind her own business, but she wanted to know what made him tick.

'Celine had never been ill in her life. She was struck down by an aneurysm.' His fingers dug into his hips, the knuckles turning white. His gaze went way beyond the waves to some place only he could see.

Wishing she hadn't caused him distress, Sarah said the first thing that came into her head. 'Do you want to take a hobble along the beach? There's time before my first patient.' She glanced down at the moon boot. 'It won't matter if I get this a bit wet.'

'Hang on, there're some plastic grocery bags in the Toyota I put over it for protection. Sand inside that thing will be a pain.' Dan went to get a bag and Leah clambered out of the vehicle to join him, skipping in circles as Dan slipped the bag over Sarah's foot.

Looking down as he deftly knotted it at the top and tucked the ends inside her boot, the urge to run her fingers through his thick, dark hair was almost uncontainable. Almost. He'd think her whacky if she followed through. *She'd* think she was whacky. Touching another person unasked went totally against who she was. Having never had lots of hugs or kisses, no spontaneous touches, from her parents or Oliver, she usually struggled with reaching out to people like that. And yet right now she had to fight the urge to touch Dan.

She'd seen the bleakness in his eyes and touching him would be a way of saying she was sorry he had been so badly hurt, to show she understood. Instead she shoved her hands deep into her trouser pockets, distorting the perfect line of the soft fabric. And said nothing. What could she say that wouldn't sound trite? Her brother had died, having a terrible effect on her. But to lose the love of your life? The mother of your child? Much worse.

He stood up and his gaze clashed with hers, sending warmth spiralling through her despite her muddled feelings.

'Let's go.' He began striding down the hard sand, leaving her to follow at an uneven, slower pace.

His shoulders were hunched as he studied the ground in front of his feet, his hands clenched at his sides. A man hurting? Or angry at her again for intruding on his privacy? Keep this up and they were going to have many clashes over the coming months.

Then Leah ran up to her, pulled at Sarah's arm to free her hand. Warm, sticky fingers wrapped around Sarah's forefinger and she was tugged along the beach. Suddenly Sarah laughed. A completely unexpected laugh that relaxed the tension that had been dogging her for weeks. What was happening to her?

'Want to share the joke?' Dan stopped to wait for her. 'I could do with a good chuckle.'

'Nothing, really. It's good to be walking on the beach as though I've got nothing to worry about. I haven't done anything like this on a regular basis.' Face it, she didn't go for any sort of exercise, ever.

'Lucky you,' her companion grunted.

'Dan, give it a break.' She wouldn't let him drag her mood down, and as Leah ran off to study a dead gull she asked, 'What are you two doing today?'

'We've got a birthday party at twelve for one of Leah's preschool mates.'

'That sounds like fun.' What did adults do at those things? Play pass-the-parcel with the kids or hide in the kitchen, drinking wine? She knew which she'd be best at and it had nothing to do with parcels.

Dan jerked his head around to glare at her. 'Fun? Fun? Lady, what do you do for entertainment if you think spending hours with a bunch of four-year-olds is fun? Want to swap places?'

They were on the same wavelength—sort of. 'Okay, it's fun for Leah, but I'm sure you'll manage to raise a smile or two of your own.'

'Why would I want to do that?' But his eyes twinkled briefly. If only he knew how gorgeous and sexy and wonderful he looked when that twinkle appeared. 'At least I won't get a sore butt today.' He ran his hands down his thighs. 'Remind me again how great a time I had riding that bolshy horse. I'm sure Bea gave me Jumbo deliberately.'

'You need Deep Heat rubbed into your muscles.' Uh-oh.

The tip of his tongue appeared between his lips. His eyes widened, darkened. 'What are you suggesting? Massaging my thighs?'

She'd prefer his backside. Oh, great. Prize idiot. If he read her mind he'd think she was making a pass at him. Again. Charging along the beach as fast as her foot allowed, she said loudly, 'So no more riding?'

'We're going again tomorrow. I think Bea has a sadistic streak that I'm only just learning about.'

'You could say you're washing your hair.' Sarah grinned, thankful the subject of rubbing his muscles had been got past even if a very definite picture of her hands on that backside remained uppermost in her head.

'Can you see Leah letting me get away with that?' He kicked a small pebble into the froth surging at the water's edge. 'Seriously, do you think you're going to enjoy your time here? Yesterday, on my way to the supermarket, I tried to see Port Weston through your eyes and I must admit the town looks a little scruffy. The tired, weatherboard buildings, the shopfronts that belong to another generation. It's not flash.'

'I wasn't expecting a miniature Auckland. I'd have stayed at home otherwise.'

'So why did you take up the contract? I mean, you're a partner in a big, modern clinic. If you wanted a change, why not cruising somewhere like the Caribbean?'

'My father talked me into taking a break.' The words slipped out without thought.

'This is a break?' He shrugged his shoulders. 'Doing my job is a holiday?'

Damn, did he think she was mocking him? 'Not at all. It's just that it's so different working here. New people, total change of scenery. Hopefully not so competitive.' So much for self-control. Around Dan it was always disappearing. 'I'd been putting in extremely long hours.'

'Why? There must be enough surgeons lining up to work with your father to last his lifetime. His reputation is awesome. You could've backed off the hours.'

And then what would she have done? How would she have filled in the time and blocked out the pain caused by

Oliver? 'I wanted to do the hours. There were things going on in my life I was ignoring.'

'I can certainly sympathise with that sentiment.' Dan sighed. 'The exact same reasons I'm now on leave. I tended to spend time with my patients rather than deal with Leah and all her problems. Because she didn't react well to my way of dealing with her distress, hasn't ever since her mother died. Family kept stepping in and helping out, taking Leah home and making her happy for a while.' He shrugged. 'It all just became so much easier to leave them all to it and I could get on with building up the hospital's surgical unit.'

'Dan, you're great with Leah. She seems so happy and well adjusted.'

'I wish you hadn't said that.' Dan winced.

'Think I'm tempting fate? That now she'll be a little hellion? I can't see it. She's so sweet.'

'You can be quite supportive, did you know that? I could get used to having you around,' he growled, but his mouth lifted at the corners.

She stared at him. 'You'd better not. I don't intend staying on past the end of March.'

He shrugged. 'Fair enough. So what were you working so hard to avoid?'

'Not avoid,' Sarah grumbled, not wanting to go there. But Dan had shared some of his story with her. It seemed natural to return the favour. 'Actually, you're right. That's exactly what I was doing. I should be in Paris right now on my honeymoon.'

Dan's eyes widened. 'Really? It'd be very cold over there at this time of the year.'

Good, a spiteful little voice squeaked in her head. 'I was supposed to get married at the beginning of December but my fiancé called it off six months ago. He was having an affair with one of the clinic's nurses, which resulted in the baby they're expecting.'

'Whoever the guy is, he doesn't deserve you. That's a lousy thing for any man to do. Didn't he have the gumption to come to you from the moment he decided the nurse was the centre of his attention?' Dan looked hurt on her behalf. Which felt good, in an odd way.

'Oliver's also a partner in my father's surgical hospital, which kind of complicates things.' There was an understatement. 'Thankfully the nurse was more than happy to give up work once she learned she was pregnant.'

'Unlike you. You'd want to keep your career on track.' His eyes bored into hers.

'Yes, I would. But I believe I'd have managed to balance a family with work.' She'd have cut back her hours, certainly not spent evenings away lecturing or studying, as her father had done. 'Anyway, it doesn't matter now. I'm single and can remain focused entirely on my career.'

'What about love, Sarah? Surely you haven't cut yourself off from that happening. The kind of love that melts your heart, makes you jump out of burning buildings, brings you home every night? Don't you want to try for that again? And what about kids?'

Of course she wanted all that. Some time in the future. It was still too soon, although she already felt more at ease about her situation than she ever had.

'Time I went to work.' She spun back the way they'd come. Her foot jagged, the pain taking her breath away. What had happened to being careful?

Dan had happened. That's what. So distracting, so annoying, so endearing, that's what. He had her so mixed up emotionally it could take months to get back on an even keel. And now he'd taken her elbow to lead her slowly back to the car, ever mindful of her foot.

Emma was full of beans when Sarah hobbled into the ward, Dan beside her, his hand hovering on her elbow.

'I can manage from here,' Sarah muttered, desperate for a break from those sensual fingers on her skin. The tension she'd hoped to dispel while walking on the beach had increased beyond reason, tightening her tummy further. Instead of pushing Dan away with her revelations, they seemed to have drawn a little closer to each other. She had yet to work out if that was a good thing. 'I could've managed from the car park.'

'I've got half an hour to fill in.' Dan shrugged away her annoyance as if he didn't care what she thought. Which he probably didn't.

'You must have something else to do, something that has nothing to do with the hospital or patients.' She ground out the words through clenched teeth. Why had he come here? To check out her patient skills? Or did he just like being with her? If she had to choose a reason she hoped it was the second. Wishful thinking. Daniel Reilly was a control freak struggling to let go of his practice.

Jerking out of his grasp, Sarah waved to Emma across the room. Dressed in blue shorts and a T-shirt covered in bright pink daisies with flaming red centres, she looked a picture of happiness and health.

'Hi, Dr Sarah. I'm going home today.'

'Emma, sit still for a moment.' Gayle Duncan tried to grab hold of her daughter. Not a chance. 'Sorry, Sarah, but she's so happy to be getting out of here.'

'Who can blame her for that?' Sarah had got to know

Gayle quite well while she'd spent the days since Emma's appendectomy reading or playing games with her daughter.

Just as she would in the same situation. The thought slammed into Sarah's brain. Tick tock went the biological clock. She bit down on her bottom lip, desperately wanting this uncalled-for need to go away. Why now? Why here? Her gaze went straight to Dan standing on the other side of the bed, his thoughtful expression focused directly on her. Uh-oh. Did he have anything to do with this need? No way. He might be very attractive and distracting but what she felt for him was plain old lust. Certainly not grounds for considering having babies with the guy.

'Dr Dan, is your holiday finished?' Emma bobbed up and down before him.

He was slow to look away from Sarah to the girl trying to get his attention, and Sarah worried that she'd given away too much in those brief moments. He seemed able to see past all her defences right to her real wants and needs. Almost as though he knew her better than she did.

Which made him very dangerous to be around.

'Not yet. I brought Dr Livingston in and soon I'm going to pick up Leah from the library reading morning.'

So go. Get out of here. Give me space to gather my thoughts and put my head back in order. Sarah sent silent messages to him but he didn't move. *That's right, be obtuse. You were reading my mind fine before.*

'I'm going to play outside when I get home,' Emma told him.

Gayle asked Sarah, 'Do you want to check Emma before we go?'

Sarah scanned Emma's charts and notes. 'Everything looks absolutely fine. My main concern was Emma's temperature. As that's now completely normal you can take her home and spoil her.'

Sitting on the edge of the bed, Sarah patted the covers beside her. 'Emma, I want you to do something for me. Your tummy has been very sick so you have to look after it for a few more days. You mustn't do rough things that might hurt it. No climbing trees or riding the bike yet.'

Gayle chipped in before Sarah could say any more. 'Careful. This calls for reverse psychology. A certain young lady will immediately do anything you tell her not to.'

'I'll be very, very good. Won't I, Mummy?' Those enormous brown eyes were turned on Gayle.

Sarah chuckled. 'I don't know how you can say no to her.' She'd make a hopeless parent, spoiling any children she had. Children. Plural. Thinking of more than one child now? Unbidden, her longing swamped her, making her powerless to move. Then Emma leaned close to place a damp kiss on her chin, causing Sarah's eyes to mist over. Wordlessly she reached for Emma, gave her a quick hug.

She had to get out of here. She was making an idiot of herself. Getting all teary and giving spontaneous hugs. Next she'd be turning up to work in track pants and a T-shirt. This place sure had a way of playing havoc with everything as she knew it.

'Tell me again how I got to be at a child's birthday party?' Sarah asked Dan as they sat on the lawn, watching Leah leaping along in a sack trying to beat all the other kids to the finish line.

'You had nothing else to do.'

Sure, but a kid's party? 'I'd have found something.'

'Relax. No one's going to bite you.' Dan grinned at her discomfort, reminding her of the first morning when she'd been shocked awake by Leah crawling under the covers with her. Once the surprise had faded Sarah had enjoyed having a warm tot wriggling down beside her under the sheet.

She nudged Dan. 'Think you're needed. Leah's taken a tumble in her sack.'

'The tears will be because she hasn't won, not because she's hurt herself. Let's hope they don't last long.' He was quick to lift Leah up and set her on her feet again. 'Keep going. You've got to finish the race.'

Leah's heart wasn't in it. 'No, I'm going to sit with Sarah.'

'You've got to learn not to quit, my girl.' Dan's hands were on his hips.

'She's only four,' Sarah said. Sounding like a mother? Eek.

'Got to teach her these things right from the start.' Dan reached down to Leah as though to set her in the right direction but she ducked and slid past him, in her hurry tripping over the sack again and skidding on the rough grass.

The ensuing shrieks and cries were ear-piercing. Everyone turned to see what had happened. Two mothers rushed over to check on Leah. Dan scooped her up into his arms, holding her to his chest. 'She's all right,' he told everyone, and kissed Leah's forehead, at which point Leah squealed louder. 'Carry on with the race.'

One of the mothers remained with them while the other returned to the young partygoers and got them racing again. Leah cried louder. 'It hurts, Daddy.' And she snuggled in closer to his chest.

Panic filled Dan's eyes. He sat down on the ground, his big hand on Leah's head. 'Shh, little one. Take it easy. Where does it hurt?'

'Everywhere,' Leah answered between sobs.

Sarah was perplexed. A tumble in a sack shouldn't cause

this amount of distress. Unless… 'Does Leah suffer from any medical condition that would precipitate this reaction?'

Dan gulped. 'Ah, no. Here, can you hold her while I look her over?'

About to put her arms out to take the child, Sarah hesitated. Why the panic in Dan's eyes if there wasn't a condition to worry about? What upset him so much? Leah needed him more than anyone else. Light-bulb moment. That was the problem. He was afraid he couldn't comfort her. 'No, Dan, it's you Leah wants.' Sarah knelt down beside them. 'I'll look her over while you hold her.'

Dan's eyes darkened with disappointment and something like fear. He looked around, spied the mother still standing with them and began to lift Leah towards her. 'Would you?'

Sarah shook her head at the woman, silently asking her to say no. She sensed Dan had to get through this moment without letting his daughter go to someone else.

'Sarah's right, Dan. Leah needs her daddy right now.'

'But listen to her. She's not quietening down for me.'

'With some kids it takes a while.' The woman gave Sarah a knowing smile and strolled away.

'You're doing fine. I think the volume might be lowering a bit.' Sarah's heart squeezed for this big man totally out of his depth. She gently took one of Leah's arms and checked it over, then her legs. 'You've scrapped some skin off your knee, sweetheart.' And she bent to kiss it. 'There you go, all better.'

Sarah sat down beside Dan to wait while Leah slowly began to quieten down. The crying became soft sobs, then hiccups, and finally a large yawn as she settled further down into the comfort of her father's arms. And slowly the tension eased in Dan's muscles, relaxing away until he watched Leah in awe, his chest rising and falling as his breathing became settled.

Sarah swallowed around the lump in her throat. 'See, you're a great dad.'

'That's the first time I've managed to settle her when she gets that worked up.'

Leah's reaction had been out of proportion. 'Does she always do that? Get herself totally wound up?'

'Ever since her mother died and it's been up to me to comfort her.'

'I think there are two issues there, not one. It's not that you can't console her, it's that she just needs to work through her pain about her mum. You've made a habit of handing her over to others to comfort, haven't you?' *Don't do that, Dan. Your daughter loves you more than anyone else. You're her father.* There were a few things she'd like to point out to Dan but didn't want him thinking she was a know-all. And she wasn't about to tell him she had first-hand experience of a father who was never there when she really needed him.

Dan glanced across to Sarah. 'You're the first person to ever refuse to take her for me.' He gulped. 'Thank you. I think.'

Sarah forced a laugh. 'You were trying to palm her off on someone who hasn't a clue how to console an upset child. I had to do something to save her.' She leaned over and kissed the top of Leah's head, got a lungful of the heady male scent of Dan. Her eyes closed for a second before she lifted her head and placed a light kiss on Dan's cheek.

Shock rippled through her as her lips touched his freshly shaven cheek, as she inhaled the scent of him. What had she done? She jerked back, out of reach. She was crazy. Risking a glance, she saw surprise reflected in Dan's eyes.

'Daddy, what's a three-legged race?'

Thank you, Leah, now your father can concentrate on you and forget my little mistake. But Sarah rolled her lips together softly, thinking it didn't really feel like a mistake. If she wound back a few minutes to before she'd brushed her lips over Dan's cheek, would she have done it? Yes.

Dan's gaze dropped to his precious bundle. 'You tie one of your legs to someone else's and run to the finish line.'

'Can we do that? Will you run with me?' Leah asked, her eyes wide and puffy.

'This I can't wait to see.' Sarah tried for a laugh. Five minutes later the laughter was wiped off her face.

'The three-legged race is split between girls with their mothers, and boys with their fathers.' Dan studied Sarah with a big question in his eyes.

'Um, I'm not Leah's mother.' Why had she come to this party? Because Dan had talked her into doing something she didn't want to do. And now he wanted her to take part in a race with his daughter. 'Sorry, got a moon boot, remember?'

Leah's little face fell. 'We can tie the other leg to me. Please Sarah. There's chocolate for the winner.'

That face got to her. What a sucker she was turning into. How much would it hurt her foot to try? She held her hand up to Dan to be hauled off the ground. 'Go easy on me, okay?' She tickled Leah under the chin and tried to ignore Dan's fingers as they tied the ribbon around her leg.

Together with Leah she hobbled to the start line, Leah tripping over more than once. Gritting her teeth as her fractures protested, Sarah said, 'Okay, we need a plan.' And whispered in Leah's ear.

Leah wrapped her arms around Sarah's waist and put her free foot on top of the one joined to Sarah's leg. And at the blow of the whistle they were racing. Step, thump. Step, thump.

'Daddy, Sarah and me got chocolate,' Leah shrieked a few minutes later.

'Sarah and I,' Dan automatically corrected.

'Cos we were the most un-unusualist.'

'Unusual,' Dan corrected her again, before turning to Sarah. 'Thanks. You've made Leah's day.'

'It was kind of fun.' Despite her foot, and that people were looking at her funny, as though she and Dan were an item, she was enjoying herself. Quite a few women were glancing at Dan and her, questions written all over their faces. So she obviously wasn't his usual type. They needn't worry. He wasn't hers either.

'Looks like lunch is next.' Dan led them to the laden tables. 'Ready for jelly and chicken nuggets?'

'On the same plate?' Sarah shuddered.

'Live dangerously.' Dan winked.

'Sarah, do you like fairy bread?' Leah peered up at her, holding out a plate filled with bread smothered in the tiniest dots of coloured sugar.

Sarah, do you like fairy bread? she could hear her brother asking, pressing a plateful into her hand. Where had that come from? There hadn't been parties like this when she was little. Yes, there had. When she'd been about Leah's age Robbie had had a birthday party and her parents had taken them to the zoo, along with lots of other children. They'd fed the monkeys with leftover food. No way. She was in lala land. That had not happened. She'd never forget a party.

'Sarah? Are you okay?' Dan took her elbow as though he expected her to fall down in a heap.

She shook away the memory, if that's what it was, and said, 'I'm fine. And, yes, I love fairy bread.' She had thirty-something years ago anyway. *See, it's not a dream. It happened.* What else from her childhood had she forgotten? What other good, fun things had been lost in the need to impress her father and gain his attention?

CHAPTER SIX

DAN flicked the vegetable knife into the sink and snapped the cold tap on so fiercely water sprayed over the bench and across the front of his T-shirt. The walls closed in on him as he leaned back against the bench.

At the kitchen table Sarah and Leah were making cookies. Both of them had cute smudges of flour on their cheeks. Leah's eyes were enormous in her face as she followed Sarah's instructions on mixing the chocolate pieces into the dough.

'Oops!' Sarah chuckled and scooped up a handful of creamed mix from the table where it had flicked from the bowl due to Leah's over-enthusiastic stirring. 'Slow down a bit. Here.' She popped a chocolate button into Leah's grinning mouth.

'Look, Daddy, I'm mixing the biscuits.'

'You're doing a great job.' Warmth stole over him. His girl couldn't be happier. Sarah had done that for her. Antsy Sarah, who swore she knew nothing about children's needs. Sarah, who did three-legged races with a moon boot just to give a child a special moment. 'So are you, big girl.'

He got glared at with piercing green eyes. 'Big girl?'

'As in Leah's my little one.' The glare sharpened. 'Can I pour you a wine? It's that time of the day.' He opened the fridge and took out a bottle of white wine, waving it at her. Hopefully diverting her.

The green lightened, her mouth twitched. 'Yes, please.'

'Me too, Daddy.'

Dan shook his head as he poured one wine and a juice. What had happened to his plan to have dinner cooking and Leah bathed and in her PJs by now? Females, young and older, that's what had happened. Both distracting in their own way. Both taking over his kitchen and making the mother of all messes.

'Aren't you having anything?' Sarah asked as he put the bottles back in the fridge.

'Yes, actually, I am.' He'd forgotten to get himself a beer. His nice, orderly world seemed to be going all to hell. How could this woman cause so much mayhem just by being—being there? He was even starting to think that she'd make a good mother for his Leah, and that was a really, stupid idea. It would never work. He wasn't moving to Auckland with all its traffic and no green paddocks. And Sarah? Well, she'd never consider living permanently so far away from those spas and dress designers. Though those trousers she had on now weren't as posh as some of the outfits she'd worn so far. Slumming it? Snapping the tab on a can of lager, he grinned. Sarah was most definitely relaxing a bit.

'Good, I don't like drinking alone.' A smile curved her full lips. 'What are we having for dinner?' she asked.

'You're as bad as Leah. We've got fresh blue cod caught by a local fisherman.'

'Yum. How are you cooking it?'

'In the pan.' This wasn't one of her fancy restaurants where she'd get sauces and fresh herbs and other garnishes.

One corner of Sarah's delectable mouth curled upward before she asked Leah, 'Do you want to stir the nuts in now?'

'I don't like nuts.' Leah stopped poking the buttons into the mixture with her fingers. 'They're yukky.'

'Have you tried them?' Sarah looked a bit stunned.

'Not many kids Leah's age do. Could be because parents don't let them have nuts in case they choke.'

Sarah's face fell. 'I didn't think. How stupid of me. Chocolate hazelnut cookies are a favourite of mine.' She looked at Dan, lifted her shoulders in an eloquent gesture. 'I blew it, didn't I?'

'It's not a biggie, Sarah.'

'Yes, it is. I've gone and spoiled the whole thing of having fun with Leah and being able to eat the cookies together.' She leaned down and hugged Leah to her. 'I'm sorry, sweetheart.'

'Can I eat the rest of the chocolate?'

Dan shook his head at his daughter. 'You're never one to miss an opportunity, are you? I've got a suggestion.' He looked at Sarah. 'How about Leah stirs in the rest of the buttons and makes them double chocolate cookies?'

Gratitude shone back at him. 'Good thinking.'

As the mixing resumed, Dan added for Sarah's benefit, 'You didn't spoil anything. Even if a certain young lady hadn't been able to eat the biscuits, she's still having a blast. I've never cooked with her, but it is something I'd envisaged she'd do with her mother. You've started something that I might have to keep up.' When carefully sculpted eyebrows rose he added, 'Seriously, the fun is in the doing, not just the eating.'

'Thanks.' She took a big gulp of wine. 'I remember making biscuits with Gran when we stayed at her house.'

Why the surprise in her eyes? 'Didn't you enjoy it?'

'I loved it.' Another gulp. 'I'd forgotten we did that.' Then she murmured something like, 'Seems as though I've forgotten a lot of things.'

Dan wanted to ask her what her childhood had been like but twice already he'd put his size-eleven feet in his mouth when asking her personal things so he kept quiet.

Soon the cookies were in the oven and Sarah stared at the messy table. 'Guess I know what I'm doing next.'

'I'll take care of that.' It would keep him busy for half the night. He jerked a thumb at the door. 'Go and put that leg up. I bet it hurts like crazy.'

'That's to be expected.'

'I'll check it for swelling once I've finished here. You did spend a lot of time standing on it today. Not to mention the race.'

'I'm glad I opted for the moon boot. A cast would've been clunky.' She leaned her saucy hip against the kitchen table. A smattering of flour had somehow got onto her trousers, smeared over her butt.

Dan tried desperately to focus on filling a pot with spuds rather than on the mouthwatering sight at his table. The very feminine curves appealed to his male senses. More than that, his hormones were stirring up a storm. Again. Still.

'It isn't necessary for you to check my foot. I'm qualified to do my own check-ups.' Had her voice wobbled?

'Daddy check-ups my hurts.' Leah's eyes sparkled.

Dan smiled over his shoulder at Leah, warmth bubbling through him. He'd do anything to make his girl happy. Even clean up after the sex goddess. Only days into it, he seemed to be getting a handle on this full-time-dad lark. Though he'd nearly blown it when Leah had tripped in that silly sack race. The one scenario he'd been dreading since the day he'd learned he was going on leave had happened, but Sarah had forced him to face up to his insecurities. And, with no alternative, he had. And won.

He owed Sarah big time. For the first time one of Leah's crying episodes hadn't escalated into a full-blown melt-down that he couldn't manage. He'd consoled her, comforted her, and within a short time she'd been happily bouncing all over the place, not refusing to talk, and crying for hours as had happened so often in the past. *He'd* done it. Without Auntie Bea, or Jill, or the nanny. But with Sarah on the sidelines, encouraging him with her sweet smile. What about that sweet kiss she'd dropped on his cheek? It had taken his breath away.

'Daddy, can I take the plaster off my knee now? It's all better.'

'Of course you can.' He looked at his daughter, grateful of the interruption to where his thoughts were heading. 'You're a cracker kid.'

'A Christmas cracker.' Leah put one hand in Sarah's and the other in his. 'Pull me. See what's inside like a real cracker.'

'A paper hat and a plastic toy.' Sarah smiled at Leah before her gaze turned to him.

What was she thinking? She'd appeared to enjoy the baking session until she'd realised her mistake about the nuts. Did she wish she had her own family? Of course she would. Who didn't? Not anyone with a heart. Sarah might think she'd hidden hers but he'd watched her with Emma, with Anders. Sarah gave more of herself than was expected of a surgeon dealing with a young patient. She'd taken some knocks, which could explain why she tried so hard to remain aloof. She certainly coped with Leah's demands like a veteran.

'Pot's boiling over.' Sarah nodded at him.

'What?'

'Daddy, you're dreaming. The pot's too hot.'

He spun around, flicked the gas to low. Goddamn it. He *had* been daydreaming. Why wouldn't he? A beautiful woman stood in his kitchen and he hadn't had sex for a long time. What else would a bloke be doing? It had been for ever since he'd scratched that particular urge.

A town the size of Port Weston made it difficult to have a brief fling. The gossipmongers would have a field day. Mostly when he got randy as hell, he took to digging up the garden. Nothing like hard, physical work to douse the urge. The fact that his garden was extremely overgrown was testimony to how often that happened.

But it would be impossible to find any red-blooded male who wouldn't be interested in the stunning Dr Livingston. Except, maybe, this Oliver character.

He was going to have to take Leah away for some overnight trips. Living under the same roof as Sarah was akin to lighting a fire and leaping into it.

'Thought I'd give you a treat today.' Dan spoke from Sarah's office doorway.

She leaned back in her chair, shaking her head at him. Some time over the week since the baking fiasco Dan had finally managed to stop wanting to read all the patient files and going over cases with her. But occasionally he still turned up unannounced to see if she needed help with anything. 'You're going to whisk me off to a beauty clinic where I'll be pampered for hours on end.'

'I don't think so.' He looked stunned, as if that was an odd suggestion.

'Not my lucky day, then, is it?' She smiled to soften her words.

'What about a real coffee in a real café? If you're not busy, that is? It's time you met George and Robert.'

'Sounds wonderful.' She glanced at her day planner. 'As you know full well, I'm not exactly rushed off my feet.'

'Come Monday you will be. That's a heavy schedule you've got so let's make the most of today's opportunity while we can.' His mouth twisted in a sheepish manner when she raised an eyebrow at him. 'I happened to see the operating list when I stopped to say hello to Jill.'

'Left it lying around, did we?' The list had been in a drawer at Jill's desk half an hour ago.

'I was looking for a pen.' Then he shrugged and gave her a rare grin, one that hit her right in the belly and had her wanting to know more about him. 'All right. I can't help myself. I'm an interfering beaver, I know. But for the record, you're doing a brilliant job and I couldn't have asked for a better replacement.'

About to get out of her chair, Sarah found her arms didn't have the strength to push her up. 'You what?' *Close your mouth, you're looking like a fish out of water. I feel like one.*

Dan jerked a thumb over his shoulder. 'You want that coffee or not?'

'I guess,' she croaked. She'd been paid a compliment. By Daniel Reilly. What had brought that on? Mr Grumpy had more sides to him than a hexagonal block. Or else he wanted something from her.

The ride to Port Weston's main street was a silent one. Sarah dwelt on what Dan might want and as he pulled his Land Cruiser into a park outside the café she decided she'd been a bit harsh. As far as she'd noted, Dan didn't do devious so there probably wasn't any ulterior motive behind that statement. He'd meant it. And he was taking her out. Not on a date, as such, but they were going for coffee where they'd be seen by locals. So when he came around to open her door and help her down she gave him a full-beam smile. Which seemed to fluster him completely.

Inside the café he pulled out a chair for her, then waved to the two men working behind the counter. 'Robert, George, can we have some coffee please? And you'd better meet Sarah.'

Watching the men hurrying to the table, Sarah grinned. 'Seems you're popular.'

Dan twisted his mouth sideways in that wry way of his. 'It's you they want to meet. You're about to get a thorough going over.'

'Like a bag of coffee beans, you mean?'

Dan merely raised his dark eyebrows. 'Something like that.'

The shorter of the two men touched her lightly on the shoulder. 'I'm Robert, and this is my partner, George.'

George held out his hand. 'Pleased to meet you.'

She shook hands with both men.

'Your reputation has gone before you.' Robert took a long look at her.

'What am I reputed to have done?' Sarah asked, intrigued despite herself.

'It's nothing to do with what you've done, apart from falling down the pub's steps. Talk about making a grand entrance to our little community.' Robert paused, then, 'Everyone's talking about the new surgeon and her absolutely fabulous car, not to mention her exquisite clothes.'

Leaning sideways, Robert appraised her stylish mid-calf, café-au-lait-coloured trousers and peach sleeveless shirt. 'I'd have to agree. Very classy.'

Dan leaned back on his chair, arms folded across his chest, a well-worn black T-shirt stretched too tight across his muscular frame. 'Not like me at all.' And the damned man winked at her.

Sarah tried to ignore that wide chest and failed. Miserably. Her mouth dried. She itched to slip her hands between the fabric and his skin. As her stomach did a flip she wondered how she could think like this when the man annoyed the daylights out of her most of the time. Somehow, despite that, contemplating those muscles under his shirt kept her awake most nights until the sound of the sea worked its magic on her.

Wasn't she supposed to be grieving over a broken engagement? Yet here she was, drooling over the first man she'd spent any time with since Oliver. Looking up at his face, she was shocked to see him watching her. Heat pooled in the pit of her stomach as something dark and dangerous glittered back at her.

Finally Dan waved a hand. 'Hey, there, Robert, could we have some coffees? Today would be good.'

Robert rolled his eyes. 'This is what happens when you try keeping Sarah all to yourself. But we can't have her thinking we can't match it with the city types so excellent coffee coming up.'

Keeping her all to himself? Not likely. He'd taken her to that birthday party, hadn't he? Hardly the social event of the year, but there had been lots of mothers there. Not her scene at all and yet she'd had fun.

Sarah leaned her elbows on the table and dropped her chin into her hand. 'How long have George and Robert been living in Port Weston?' she asked, while her mind was still on Dan.

'About five years. Robert's a West Coaster, originally from further south in Hokitika.'

'He limps quite badly, and seems to be in some pain.' Sarah had noted the sideways drag and occasional grimace when he'd approached their table.

'He snapped a tendon and, despite surgery to reattach it,

he's had nothing but trouble since. Don't waste your breath suggesting a second operation. He's adamant he's not having one,' Dan explained. 'I've tried countless times to get him to see an orthopaedic surgeon I can recommend.'

'That's sad when he possibly could be walking around pain free.' Sarah wondered why Robert felt so strongly against a repeat op. 'Did something happen during surgery?'

Leaning his chin on his chest, Dan murmured, 'He's not saying. It was done in Christchurch but without his permission I can't request his file.'

'Has George said anything to you?'

Dan shook his head. 'He's promised Robert he won't, though I think he's bursting to discuss it. See if you can get anything out of him once you've been here a little while.'

If Dan couldn't convince Robert when he knew them so well, she didn't stand a chance. Sarah twisted around to look out the window onto the street and the people wandering past, all dressed very casually. Despite the summer temperature, many of the men wore gumboots or heavy work boots, and some people had caps on to keep the sun off their faces.

She couldn't get much further from the fashionable, bustling crowds of downtown Auckland. But if she'd been back there she'd have been tense, tapping the floor with the toe of her shoe, in a hurry to down her coffee and get back to work. Not a lot of enjoyment in that, while here she was happy to take her time, savouring the company, and hopefully the coffee when it came.

Robert placed their cups on the table, turned to Sarah. 'I hear there's a roster for driving you to the hospital.'

'There is. It astonishes me how total strangers are waiting outside the gate in the morning, ready to drive me to work. The same thing happens when it's time to go home.'

'That's what living on the Coast is all about, helping one another,' Robert said.

Even at three o'clock that morning someone had picked her up when she'd been called in to an emergency. She hoped it wasn't part of their 'keep Dr Sarah here' plan, which she'd heard about through the hospital grapevine.

She'd be disappointing the board about that. Although she'd begun appreciating the friendliness of everyone, and their genuine enquiries about how she was coping, the reality was that this place did frustrate her at times. Yesterday had been a prime example.

Turning to Dan, she said, 'I ordered a book from the local stationery shop, and they told me it would be a week before it arrived. A week!'

'So?' Dan drawled.

'So in Auckland it would arrive overnight. What are they doing? Writing the thing longhand?'

'Get used to it. That's how it is around here.'

'Be glad it's only a book you want.' Robert chuckled from the next table where he was wiping the surface. 'The bench top for our new kitchen took two months.'

Sarah pulled a face. And people seriously thought they could persuade her to stay? Apart from the fact that she had a partnership at the clinic to go back to, one she'd barely given a thought to since she'd arrived, she realised with a start, there was nothing in this sleepy hollow that attracted her. Not even its exceptionally up-to-date surgical unit.

What about a certain surgeon with the gentlest touch whenever he took her elbow to guide her around some obstacle? The man's startling blue eyes seemed to follow her every move. Was Dan a man who could possibly be trusted? Whoa. That was going too far. She didn't know him well enough to make that assumption. She'd known

Oliver a long time and still hadn't seen his infidelity coming.

She tapped her forehead in a feeble attempt to dash Dan from her thoughts. Impossible when he was sitting opposite her, those very blue eyes watching her.

'Sorry to gatecrash this cosy scene.' Jill loomed into Sarah's peripheral vision. 'But I've got to tell Dan my news.' Jill was bobbing up and down on her toes, grinning from ear to ear, her eyes glowing like coals on a fire.

'Jill? What is it?' Sarah looked from her new friend to Dan and saw a surprised kind of excitement lightening his face. 'Someone tell me what's going on.'

'I'm pregnant.'

'I'd say she's pregnant.'

They spoke in unison. Then Dan was out of his chair and swooping his sister-in-law into his arms and swinging her around in a circle, nearly colliding with the next table. 'Aren't you?'

'Yes, yes, yes.' Jill's eyes brimmed and fat tears spilled down her cheeks as Dan gently let her down again. 'Yes.' She squeezed her hands into fists and shook them with glee.

'That's wonderful. I'm thrilled for you.' Sarah got up to hug Jill. Oops, she didn't do hugs. Too late. And it felt good.

'We've been trying for well over a year. Malcolm and I were beginning to think we'd never be parents.' Jill danced on the spot. 'I intended keeping it a secret for a few weeks in case something went wrong.' She faltered for a moment. 'But we couldn't. So here I am, making sure you're one of the first to know, Dan.'

Dan wrapped his arms around her again, rested his chin on her head. 'Thank you, sis. I've been hoping for this news for so long, you've made my day. You really have.

And now I suppose I'd better give that brother of mine a call. He'll be busting a valve with excitement.' He tugged his phone out of his pocket.

'A call?' Jill laughed. 'He'll want a party.'

'That can be arranged.' Dan grinned. 'Yes, that's exactly what I'll do. Leave it all to me.'

Jill dropped into a chair beside Sarah, and a cup of coffee appeared at her elbow.

'Congratulations, Jill.' Robert hugged her too.

Sarah smiled as if it was the most wonderful news she'd ever heard. 'When did you actually find out?'

'First thing this morning I was banging on the door of the pharmacy before they opened. I'm late but at first I was afraid to do the test. I didn't want to find out it was a hiccup with my system. Malcolm and I agreed we'd wait until I was at least two weeks overdue.'

'How did you manage that?'

Jill hugged herself. 'We didn't. That's why I had to go get a test kit. Two weeks aren't up yet.'

Sarah grinned. 'That's better. I'd never be able to wait. I'm thrilled for you.' She really meant it. So why the gloomy sensation seeping through her? Everyone except her was having babies.

Thankfully her pager beeped. 'Guess that's the end of my break.' She read the message. 'Yep, I'm needed in A and E.' She drained her superb coffee and pushed away from the table.

Dan snapped his phone shut after a cheeky quip to Malcolm about being an old father, and said to Sarah, 'I'll drive you back and come in to see what's up. I've still got time to fill in before Leah's library session finishes.'

'Then go and see Malcolm.'

'Can't. He's got a beer tanker being unloaded, and the freight truck's due in any minute.'

There had to be something he could do rather than hang around with her. 'Then go shopping or something.'

His eyes rolled in that annoying manner. 'Shopping? Me? What for?'

'I don't know. How about some new clothes? Or groceries?' Anything, but get out of her hair, give her some breathing space. She was getting too used to him hanging around, found herself looking for him whenever he was away for very long.

Dan was still shaking his head at her suggestion as he pulled away from the café and turned back to the hospital. Then he lightly slapped the steering-wheel. 'Actually, you're right. I'll go to the shops and get something for Jill and Malcolm to celebrate their news.'

'Lovely idea.' Why hadn't she thought of that? She'd arrange for some flowers to be delivered to Jill at the pub. And she must remember to pick up a new platter from the gift shop to replace the chipped one at home.

'Malcolm's stoked.' He slowed for a truck pulling out of a side street. 'It's kind of neat we're having another child in the family. Leah's going to be so excited. A new cousin.'

'Isn't she just?' Sarah tried not to feel like even more of an outsider than she was. But it was hard to deny the twinge of envy. Dan's family had such strong bonds of love tying them all together. Unlike hers.

'I'd have loved more babies but Celine kept miscarrying.' Dan's smile dimmed briefly.

'It's not too late.' She swallowed. 'I mean, you could remarry and before you know it you'll have kids from here to Christmas.'

'Really? Now, there's a thought. Were you thinking of next Christmas?' He recovered quickly. Jill's news had made him happy. She'd have thought it would have made him sad, bringing back all those memories of Celine and the family they'd planned.

'That might take some fast work on your behalf. Unless you've already got a woman in mind.' Did he have a woman friend out there that she knew nothing about? Why wouldn't he? He was a very attractive man with a lot going for him.

'When have I had the time to date?'

'Where there's a will there's a way. Or so they say.' Relief trickled through Sarah, lifting her spirits. Something she shouldn't be feeling. She and Dan were never going to have a relationship, at least not one that led to babies. And if he was intent on having another family, he wouldn't want to be wasting time on a fling with her.

'What about you? You're not going to let that ex-fiancé spoil your chances, are you?' His eyes were fixed on the road ahead.

'Give me time to get over him before suggesting I find another man to have babies with. There's the little matter of falling in love with someone first.' But when had she last thought about Oliver? Certainly not at all today so far. He didn't keep her awake at nights any more either.

Dan did.

Dan said casually as he pulled up outside the hospital's main entrance, 'Don't take too long mending that broken heart of yours. It's holding you back from getting the most out of life.'

Her mouth fell open. 'Like what?' She shoved her door wide and snatched up her handbag. 'I've still got a lot: a fantastic apartment, my partnership in the clinic, a great job. More than enough to fill my days.' Even she found it hard to get excited about that picture.

'By the way,' he called out his window as she headed up the hospital steps, 'you'd make a wonderful mum.'

CHAPTER SEVEN

'I'M OUT in the spa,' Dan called out to Sarah as she came through the front door that evening.

And when she stepped out onto the deck he heard her faint gasp. 'That looks wonderful.'

'Come and join me.' Would she? Suddenly he was silently begging to whatever was out there that made these things happen. *Please make her want to soak in the hot water. Please.* 'The warmth works wonders on tense muscles.'

'I'm not tense.' Her teeth nibbled her lip.

Sure you're not. 'We can have dinner any time. It's all prepared.'

'Maybe I'll take a stroll along the beach instead. I've had a big day.'

Yep. I can see your tight shoulders, your tired eyes.

Just then a gust of wind blew through the trees, filling the air with the sound of rustling leaves. *Thank you.* Dan grinned. 'There's rain coming.'

Her eyebrows rose in that delightful way she had. 'I'll go change into my swimsuit.'

Thank goodness she'd packed a swimsuit. He'd have blown a gasket if she'd told him she was coming in naked. When she wandered out five minutes later he still nearly blew one. Her simple black costume fitted superbly, outlining those full breasts to perfection, accentuating the curves of her hips. Her flat stomach sent his into spasms. He could not take his eyes off her as she climbed into the bubbling water and sat beside him.

Beside him? Being in the spa with Sarah suddenly became a really, really bad idea. His blood pressure started rising. What was wrong with him? Of course. Blame Sarah for being so delectable.

Clearing his throat, he tried to sound nonchalant. 'Would you like a wine?'

She glanced at the low table beside the spa where two glasses and a bottle stood next to a plate of crackers and Brie. Again her eyebrows rose, and her mouth twitched. 'A very small one.'

Stupid, stupid. Dan berated himself as he poured her drink. She must think he was seducing her. That's how it looked from here. He'd wanted everything seeming effortless so she wouldn't think anything of it when he suggested she join him. Went to show how out of practice at entertaining women he'd become. He was more like the new kid at kindergarten with all the unfamiliar toys and too frightened to touch any of them than a confident man and father of one.

Right now he should be leaping out of the spa, putting distance between them. Then she'd think him a really hopeless case. He'd stay put, but for the life of him he didn't know how he was going to keep his hands to himself.

Sarah slid deep into the warm water, letting the bubbles roll up her back, around her neck. Her eyes closed and she smiled. 'This has to be the best invention ever.'

He passed over her glass. 'Keep an ear out for the oven timer. I've got some muffins baking for tomorrow.' Keep the conversation on normal, everyday things and he might survive the next half-hour without making a complete fool of himself.

'You and Leah going somewhere that you need muffins?'

'Depending on the weather we might head to the river for a swim.' Dan studied her over the rim of his glass. Something was bothering her. Occasionally over the last few days he'd seen her wandering along the beach, hands in her pockets, chin on her chest, deep in thought. And when she'd come back those beautiful big eyes had been dark with sadness, and he'd want to haul her into his arms and hug her tight. Like he would for any of his family. That look was there now.

Sarah isn't family. Sarah's a hot woman whom you'd like to bed. There is a difference, man. Couldn't he bed her and help her at the same time?

'You're enjoying your time off now, aren't you?' She sounded wistful. 'Having a great time with Leah.'

'Absolutely. I wish I'd done it ages ago. Who knows what I've missed out on with my girl? If I ever have any more kids, I'll definitely be there all the time, not hiding at work.'

'You said you wanted more children. Got a number in mind?'

He tasted his wine and looked out beyond the end of the lawn to where he could hear the waves pounding their relentless rhythm. 'There was a time I wanted four.'

'Four?' She smiled. 'You're a devil for punishment.'

'I've always been surrounded by people. I can't imagine life without siblings and I want the same for Leah. Celine and I were trying but she kept miscarrying. Five times. The doctors couldn't explain it. We saw everyone, and I mean everyone. Specialists here and in Australia. The more we were told there was no obvious reason, the more

Celine blamed herself. Nothing I said made the slightest bit of difference.'

'That must have been hard for you both.'

'Very.'

'How did Celine cope?'

'At first she was distraught, as any woman would be. I admit, so was I. But after each miscarriage she became moodier, filled with despair, spiralling into a black hole that no one could coax her out of.' He gulped at his drink. He recalled those dark nights and days, trying to make Celine understand that he was happy with their small family; that she and Leah were precious to him. She'd argued she wasn't good enough for him because she couldn't give him what he wanted. That had hurt. Badly. 'Not even me. Heaven knows, I tried.'

Movement in the water and Sarah leaned closer to lay her hand on his arm. She didn't say anything, just touched him.

He took her hand in his and sat there looking at the woman who was changing so much for him. Her determination to carry on even when her foot hurt, her cheerful manner, her sweet smile, the way she was always ready to listen, even her occasional crankiness—all these things and more were helping him get back a life he'd forgotten existed. A life that looked pretty darned good from where he sat. As did his companion. Her cheeks had coloured to a soft pink, and the tiredness staining her face had vanished.

When Sarah turned to place her glass on the table her gaze clashed with his. Without thought he caught her arms and tugged her gently towards him just as she leaned forward. They slid off their seats. Dan instinctively wrapped his arms around her, holding her to his chest, as they bobbed in the bubbling water.

Sarah slid her arms around his waist. Her hands spread out over his back. He could feel each fingertip where they pressed lightly on his skin. The swirling water and her touch were a sensual mix of satin and silk, of soft and firm. He'd arrived in heaven.

His lungs suspended all breathing while his mind assimilated the feel of Sarah's slick, warm skin under his palms. He moved closer, placed his lips on her throat. Her pulse thumped under his mouth, and he could feel her throbbing response in the fingers that were now pushing through his hair, beating a feverish massage on his scalp. Heard it in the hiss of her indrawn breath.

His tongue traced a line under her chin and up to the corner of her mouth, where he teased her lips gently with his teeth, warming the cooler flesh. He lost all sense of time, place, everything—except Sarah, and he couldn't get enough of her. Her mouth, when he tasted it, was sweet with wine. An outpouring of exquisite sensations overtook him.

Then she touched his face, held his head closer, and kissed him back with all the fierceness of a starved woman. He didn't, couldn't, stop to question what was behind her actions. Her need fired his own to an even deeper level and he leaned further into her, his bones melting.

On the periphery he thought he heard something. What? Ignoring it, his mind sank back into the pool of whirling sensations Sarah stirred up.

Beep. Beep. Beep.

He dragged his mouth away from those wondrous lips. Cocked his head to one side. Every swear word he could think of flicked through his mind as he tried to blink his eyes into focus.

'What?' Sarah croaked.

'The goddamned muffins are ready.'

'Let them burn.'

'You want the fire brigade turning up?'

Dan swore under his breath. The kitchen floor was slippery with water that had dripped from his shorts when he'd charged inside to save the wretched muffins. He fetched a mop and began cleaning up, at the same time trying to put that kiss into perspective. Yeah, right. Like how? When his body was in a state of expectation, turned on as quickly as a flick of a switch. Unfortunately it couldn't be turned off as swiftly.

Sarah walked through from outside, quietly, as though hoping he wouldn't notice her. She'd have to be invisible for that to happen. And not wear that special fragrance of hers.

'Sarah?' he couldn't resist calling in a low voice as she passed. He did not want her to ignore what had just happened between them. That kiss had been as real as the waves pounding the beach across the road. And as hard to hold onto. Especially if Sarah decided to pretend it had been a passing clashing of lips with nothing more to it.

'I'm going to have a shower and head to bed. It's been a long day.' The yellow of her towel highlighted the gold flecks in her eyes when she met his gaze.

He couldn't read her. 'You don't want tea and a muffin?' She always had a cup of tea and something sweet to eat before retiring. 'You haven't had dinner.'

'No, thanks.' She was rejecting him—after that heart-stopping kiss.

A chill lifted bumps on his arms. The depth of his yearning shocked him. Whatever they'd started must not stop. He wanted more from her, much more. So he should be grateful this was as far as it was going, should be glad one of them had the sense to put the brakes on before it got out of hand.

But he'd begun to enjoy having Sarah here, in his house, his hospital. In his life. He woke up in the mornings feeling happier than he had in years and he didn't believe that was only because he was on leave with his daughter. He grimaced. Even if making daisy chains had been a novel way of filling in an afternoon. No, he enjoyed having another adult at home to talk with, to share meals with.

Get real. You enjoy having a very hot woman under your roof and you're only biding your time until she's under your sheets.

He managed to say something sane and sensible. 'Goodnight.'

Her relief was almost palpable as she paused. 'Goodnight, Dan.' Her fragrance reminded him of the scent of lavender on a gentle breeze. 'I'm, um, sorry we were interrupted.'

'What?' Talk about mixed messages.

'But I think it's for the best. We've got to live together for quite a while and if we'd carried on it would only have made life very difficult for us.'

Okay, not mixed. Clear as day. He gripped his hips in an attempt to stop reaching out to touch her. To stop from running his fingers behind her ear and down beneath her chin, over the fair skin of her throat. He yearned to kiss away that frown, to make her mouth soft and pliant under his again.

'Yes, you're right.' Damn it. She was. An affair might solve the immediate problem of needing sex, but Sarah was still hurting from what that other character had done to her. She needed time, patience and care before she was ready for something as hot and casual as a fling with him. But now he'd tasted her it had become even harder to ignore the frisson of tension she whipped up in him.

The Jaguar crawled along, the big engine purring. Thankfully Sarah's foot had pretty much returned to normal, allowing her the luxury of driving again. As long as she didn't go jogging or anything equally mad.

What a busy week with long hours, though nothing like the pressure she worked under back home. She hadn't seen a lot of Dan since that kiss. As though he was staying well away from her.

Tonight, knowing she didn't have to be up at the crack of dawn, she'd relax with a glass of wine, cook a meal that did not involve satisfying a four-year-old palate, and watch a good crime programme on TV. Something that didn't involve a red-blooded male's idea of good television, meaning cricket or any other sport.

Turning into the drive, her foot lifted off the accelerator as disappointment enveloped her. Vehicles were parked haphazardly between the gate and the house. Worse, people, lots of them, were gathered on the lawn and the deck.

'There goes the poached salmon.' Sarah eased the Jag between Dan's Land Cruiser and a small truck. Gathering up her groceries, she eased open the door. Laughter and voices carried to her, Leah's shrieks outdoing them all. Reaching back into the car, she lifted up the bunch of roses and the twisted glass vase she'd purchased that afternoon at the florist next to the café. The house needed a sparkle put into it.

'Can I carry those for you?'

She jerked around at Dan's question. 'Sure. Are we having a party?'

Guilt clouded his eyes to almost black. 'Sorry. I

should've warned you.' He waved a hand towards the over-crowded deck.

'So all these people…' she nodded '…just turned up?'

'Not exactly. Remember I told Jill I'd give Malcolm a party to celebrate the pregnancy? Well, she decided tonight was the night.' His hand brushed hers as he took the grocery bags.

The familiar tug of heat stopped whatever she'd been about to say. No matter that they'd managed to avoid each other most of the week, the desire their kiss awakened had only been tamped down, not put out.

Obviously Dan wasn't affected in the same way because he was strolling up the drive, explaining what had happened. 'This is way bigger than I'd intended. Malcolm's to blame. He took it into his head to organise someone to run the pub tonight and then invited half the patrons here.' Dan didn't look at all repentant.

'Right.' With her body shivering and shimmying with desire it was difficult to concentrate on what Dan was saying as she walked beside him. 'You must've spent the whole day preparing food.' There'd been next to nothing in the fridge that morning when she'd got her breakfast and she could see a large table laden with containers of food.

'That's just it. They all know me enough to bring food with them. I've been working on the section all day—mowing, weeding, trimming trees. No time for the supermarket.'

Sarah looked around, for the first time noticing how cared for the property looked. 'You have been busy. The place looks wonderful.'

Dan growled, 'I probably shouldn't have started. Now I'll have to keep it looking like this. I'd forgotten how much effort it takes. It's years since I gave a hoot about gardens and lawns, but when today dawned sunny and calm I made the most of the opportunity to get stuck in.'

'Don't tell me you're a surfer from way back?' She pointed to a surfboard leaning against the shed. Her mouth dried as she pictured Dan in swimming shorts, his legs braced on the board as he rode a wave, balanced by those strong arms.

'Like the horse riding, it's been years. But I'm going to give it a crack over the next few days. More sore muscles coming up.' He smiled at her. 'And there's something else I'd obviously forgotten.'

'What's that?'

'How to have fun. I can thank you for my awakening.'

'How's that?' Leah made better conversation than she did.

He pointed to the flowers. 'You make our house feel like a home again.' Dan flicked out a second finger. 'I'm enjoying cooking for cooking's sake. It's no longer a chore to be done as quickly and effortlessly as possible. And I spend more time on the deck watching sunsets and sunrises than I've ever done. It's great.'

He was crediting her with that? He needed his head read. She'd contributed less than zilch to the way he got on with his life. 'You're on leave and finally relaxing.'

The third finger popped up. 'It dawned on me today when I began poking around in the shed that there's a lot more to do than work, work and work.'

'There's Leah.' Could she learn a thing or two from Dan? Find something else to do other than work? Like what? Sport? Knitting? Flower decorating? Nothing rang any bells of excitement. She'd never spent time playing.

'And there's me.' Dan spun around in front of her. 'No one is going to be me, do my things—except me. So let's get rid of these bags and party.'

Right. Sure. Surely his plans for living didn't include her?

'Sarah, there you are.' Jill approached to give her a hug. 'You're becoming a bit like Dan, all work and no play. Come and meet the rest of the mob.'

'I thought it was a family affair.' Not Dan's comingout party. 'Is there anyone left in town?'

Jill rolled her eyes. 'This is family, sort of. These Reillys are a prolific lot.'

Dan retorted, 'Especially since Malcolm has finally worked out how it's done. I'm looking forward to meeting the newest member of our clan.'

Jill laughed. 'You've got eight months to wait.'

Sarah grinned. 'Eight months. You're obviously counting the minutes.' Did she fear something happening to her as it had to her sister? Did she ever think her child might be left motherless like Leah? If the glow on her face and the happiness in her eyes were pointers then definitely not. Besides, it must be reassuring to know someone in the extended family would look out for the child if the unimaginable happened.

Sarah moved towards the house. 'I'll go and put my bag in my room and change into something more in keeping with a barbecue.'

'No, you don't. You'll hide away and I'll have to drag you out here.' Dan followed her.

She'd been going to sit down, try to pretend that a crowd of strangers weren't outside having a great time, and that she had to meet them all. 'Five minutes?'

'Two.'

Stifling an oath, she stomped through the house, threw her handbag on the bed and quickly divested herself of her suit, replacing it with shorts and a blouse. Port Weston had turned on a superb day, which was continuing into the evening. She could do with some sun on her skin. As long as it didn't bring out the freckles.

What could she talk about to everyone? They had nothing in common with her. Everyone she'd met since arriving here had been very friendly but she stood out like a bean in a fruit salad.

'Time's up.' Dan leaned against her bedroom door.

'You ever heard of knocking?' At least her blouse was buttoned up and her shorts zippered.

'No one's going to eat you, so you can take that worried expression off your face.' So why did he look like he wanted to indulge in a little nibbling? 'And here's a glass of your favourite bubbles.' He offered her the cold glass, and as she gratefully took it, he added, 'Relax, you'll be fine. They're mostly my family.'

Exactly.

Sarah parked herself on the steps leading from the deck to the lawn and very soon a tall, slim woman joined her. 'I'm Bea, Dan's older, and apparently bossier, sister. I hope we're not overwhelming you.'

'There are quite a few of you. Especially when Jill's relatives are added into the mix.' Could she ever get used to having so many people in her life, people who would want to know her business? Want to share the ups and downs of life? Why was she even wondering about it?

'When my brothers married the two sisters, our family seemed to expand rapidly. Jill and Celine have even more family than the Reillys.' Bea glanced across the lawn. 'Speaking of children, here comes Leah, heading directly for you.'

'Me?' Sarah blinked. 'I doubt it. I hardly see her during the week. She's usually in bed by the time I get home, and I'm gone again before anyone's up.' But her heart warmed as she watched Leah racing towards her.

'Yeah, and whenever I have her she talks nonstop about you. Sarah this, Sarah that. She adores you.'

'Sarah, you came home for the party.' A bundle of arms and legs hurtled into her, knocking her glass over and tipping her back against the railing post.

'Hey, kiddo, slow down.' Automatically Sarah wrapped her arms around Leah's body to protect her. And to hug her. She did a lot of hugs these days. Then Leah plonked a sloppy kiss on her chin. Tears threatened, and Sarah blinked rapidly. Leah adored her? Her? Surely not. So why was her heart dancing?

'What did I say?' Bea winked at her. 'Seems like you're having the same effect on our Dan, too.'

'Dan's talking nonstop about me?' Bea was crazy. First Leah adored her and now she was changing Dan too. Did insanity run in the family? She glanced at Leah, a perfectly normal child if ever there was one.

Bea shook her head at Sarah. 'No. He doesn't mention you at all, not a word.'

Now she was really confused. 'I'm not following you.'

'My brother's always talking about people, mostly how useless they are at this, how bad at that. But you, nothing. His lips are sealed. Which says to me you are getting to him.' Bea stood up, and added, 'For the record, I like it. I really do.'

'You don't know me.' With her arms still wound around Leah Sarah stared up at Bea. People didn't love her, not unconditionally as Bea had suggested Leah might. 'For the record, Dan definitely isn't interested in me.'

Bea only laughed. 'I'll get you another drink while you and Leah talk about your respective days.'

'I've been helping Daddy clean the shed.' Leah wriggled around on Sarah's knees. 'We found lots of his toys.' Her little hands picked up one of Sarah's and held it tight.

Warm and sticky hands. A small, bony bottom that bounced on Sarah's thighs. Leah chattered nonstop, her sweet, freckled face lit up with an enormous smile, a smile just like those rare ones of Dan's. A lump closed Sarah's throat. Her arms gently tugged Leah a little closer. Darn, she'd miss Leah when she went away.

'Here.' Dan handed down the refilled glass. An odd look filled his eyes as he looked from his daughter to Sarah and back. 'That was a big welcome home.'

Wasn't he happy Leah had raced to see her? Sarah gulped at the bubbly, studying his face and preparing to put Leah away from her. No, she'd read Dan wrong. He looked more…confused. As though he sensed a bond growing between Leah and herself that he was unsure about. His protective instincts kicking in? Very wise. Someone had to look out for Leah's heart and Dan was the man.

Sarah put down her glass and placed Leah on the step beside her, growing cold when the contact between them broke. *And I'll look after my own heart, keep it intact, avoid too much involvement with this gorgeous man and his child.* The lump in her throat expanded. Could be she was already too late.

Bea's conversation filtered into her mind. So Dan didn't say a word about her to his sister.

She needed to get away from his looming presence to make some sense of what Bea had said. She'd mix and mingle, meet some of these people. Meet the family. Okay, jump back in her car and head somewhere, anywhere. Reaching up to the railing to haul herself onto her feet, her hand encountered Dan's and he helped her up.

'Thanks,' she muttered, and leaned down to retrieve her glass.

'You're very good with Leah. Patient and fun.' Those blue eyes locked with hers. Searching for what?

'Patience is not my strong point.' Certainly not with children. What was with these people? Pushing Leah at her as though it was normal.

Dan ran a thumb across the edge of her chin. 'You underrate yourself.' Then he repeated Bea's words. 'Leah thinks you're the best, and I'm starting to think she may be a good judge of character.'

Before Sarah could think up an answer to that, they were thankfully interrupted.

'Hello, there, Dan. Sorry we're late but Brent's truck got stuck out at the mine.'

'Cathy, you're looking good.' Dan gave the very pregnant woman a hug before introducing her to Sarah. 'And here's Brent and their daughter, Cushla. Hey, cutey-pie.' Dan chucked the girl under her chin and received a shy smile in return.

'Hi.' Sarah shook Brent's hand and smiled at the toddler with the flat facial features suggestive of Down's syndrome. 'Hello, Cushla.'

The child peeked up at her from behind her father's legs. 'Wello.'

Sarah turned back to Cathy. 'When's your baby due?' The woman appeared to be in her late thirties, maybe early forties.

'Five weeks, and counting,' Cathy rubbed her extended tummy. 'Hot days like today are very uncomfortable.'

'And you can't wait for him to arrive so you can do all those things mums do with their newborns,' Brent hugged Cathy around the shoulders. 'Cathy's a wonderful mum.'

'I just love it,' Cathy agreed. 'Now I've got to see Jill. It's so exciting. Two babies being born into our family this year.'

Sarah raised an eyebrow. 'Don't tell me you're related to the Reillys too?'

'Dan and I are cousins.'

Sarah shook her head. This went way past her idea of a big family.

Dan glanced at her. 'Always room for new blood.' His gaze slid over her, hesitating at her mouth, before he turned away.

Surely he wasn't considering her for the role? They'd shared one kiss. That was all. He could not be getting ideas of having all those extra children he wanted with her. Lighten up. That look had been more about sex than babies. Hadn't it?

Did she want Dan's babies? As Dan wandered away she glanced from him to Leah and back, her teeth nibbling her lip. Leah was gorgeous. Dan made beautiful babies. But, then, he was gorgeous too. She smiled, despite herself. This was so out of left field. They'd shared one kiss and she was thinking happy families with him.

She needed to get to know him a whole lot better before she gave in to this need building in her. But already Dan had woven a spell around her, had her looking to the future with more hope than she had been on New Year's Day. Had her father been right, pushing her to come here?

Across the lawn Dan talked with two women who'd just arrived. He was completely at ease with them, and they were laughing at something he'd said.

Dan. A likeable, reliable man. A loveable man. An excellent parent despite the problems he had to sort out with Leah. He wasn't ready for anything more exciting than an affair either. So go for one. Could she? Dared she?

A sobering thought crashed into her head. Was he trustworthy? Women gravitated to him, here, at the hospital, in the street. Could he be trusted not to stray? She thought so, especially for the duration of an affair. But she was afraid to believe so. History had taught her to be very careful about that.

CHAPTER EIGHT

SARAH sat on the deck listening to the waves slapping onto the beach, hearing Dan in the kitchen as he rinsed the remaining few glasses. The last couple had finally left at about one o'clock. Leah had been sound asleep in her bed for hours. Apart from the rattle of the dishwasher being stacked, the quiet she'd been looking forward to all day had finally settled over the house.

Stars twinkled, so much brighter here on the coast without a huge city lighting up the sky. A full moon turned the sky black and made shadows on the lawn. She stretched her legs out and tipped her head back, studying the universe, looking for familiar constellations.

Instead an image of Dan's face floated across her vision. His deep-set eyes were unreadable, his lips inviting. Reminding her of their kiss. The kiss that stole into her dreams every night, that hovered in the air whenever they were in the same room together, that filled every other minute not filled with work.

That kiss had begun undoing all her defences. Dan had kissed her as though she was to be treasured and awakened, like she was hot. Some of her lost self-esteem had begun creeping back, still fragile but there nonetheless. Being desired by a sexy man like Dan did her good. She was coming alive, and suddenly wanted to reach for more.

She'd taken to staying late at the hospital, sometimes eating in the cafeteria, striving for normality. Or calm at least. Keeping her distance from temptation. She might be thinking about wanting to take this further with Dan but she'd never put herself out there, afraid he might turn her down.

'I've made you some tea.'

Sarah jerked her head around. 'Tea?'

When she was thinking about the effects of Dan's kiss, he was making tea. Suddenly she giggled, just like Leah. This whole scene was crazy.

'Earl Grey.' Dan's look was quizzical. 'What's so funny?'

Did he think she was laughing at him? 'Tea's great. Truly.' Then the words just popped out. 'A little tame.'

And was rewarded with the sound of his sharply indrawn breath. 'You don't like tame?'

Now it was her turn to be rendered speechless. She turned back to the stars. She should leave flirting alone. She wasn't up to speed, and now she'd backed herself into a corner. One she had to get out of in a hurry. Before temptation overrode common sense.

Dan would swear Sarah wanted him as much as he wanted her. Her gaze never left him for long. Then there was the way her tongue did that quick little flick at the corner of her mouth whenever he looked at her. So what was she afraid of? Not him, surely? Getting involved? Yeah, well, that scared the hell out of him too. Which was why a fling was the answer. But was Sarah ready for that? Did he nudge her along, or give her space to come to her own conclusion? The right one for him, of course.

His hands clenched at his sides. Go do something practical and get over her. For now, anyway. Nothing was happening tonight. Stomping inside, he headed for the laundry, his brain ignoring his warning, taunting him with sensations her lips had evoked. He wanted her. In his bed.

'You're not having her.' He bit down on an expletive. But... 'But nothing.' It would be the dumbest idea to sleep with her when they had to share his house for many more weeks. Flings were exactly that—flings. Throwaways. They invariably finished. How much more uncomfortable it would be for them then, sharing the same house. Even if she did find somewhere else to stay, it was a small town, and they'd inevitably bump into each other.

The way his relatives had taken to Sarah tonight, she'd be going to every family meal, picnic, celebration for the rest of her time here. There'd be no getting away from her. And now Bea and Jill seemed intent on helping a romance blossom for him with Sarah. As though it was the most natural thing in the whole wide world. Damn their meddling. He'd have to put a stop to that.

Except he kind of liked the idea, when he thought about it. So he shouldn't think about it. But what if he convinced Sarah to stay on come the end of March? They'd be able to pursue this thing going on between them. Because something sure as hell was. He couldn't rid his head of her. Look at the way his hormones ramped up whenever she was around. And sometimes when she wasn't.

The washing-machine lid slammed back against the wall. Dan made to toss in the wet kitchen towels, and noticed Sarah's clean washing still in the bottom of the machine. She must have forgotten it. Or been in such a hurry to get away in the morning that hanging it out was rendered unimportant.

Tugging out her clothes, he tossed them into the washing basket, before putting his wash on. When he had the machine running he took Sarah's clothes and headed out to the back porch, where there was a line under the roof. That was the norm, living on the Coast. Otherwise there'd be weeks when nothing dried.

Bending down for a handful of pegs and clothes, he groaned at the lacy white pieces of fabric in his hand. Bras and a thong. He dropped them. Blew a breath up over his face. She wore thongs. His erection was back with a vengeance.

Cool sand pushed between Sarah's toes, covered her feet, as she strolled along, easily avoiding stones and driftwood in the moonlight. Down here the waves were louder. Foam spread out, pushed towards her, rolling shells over and over. Beautiful. This coastline drew her in, gave her a sense of peace when her mind was flip-flopping all over the place. She wanted Dan. She wasn't going to have him.

'You're restless tonight.' Dan spoke from behind her.

She jerked her head up, dragging her mind with her. The tension she'd been trying to ease cranked tighter. 'Why are you here?'

'I saw you wander down and thought I'd join you.'

'What about Leah? Shouldn't you be with her?'

'She's sound asleep, with Toby guarding her. If she even tries to roll over, that dog will make such a racket I'll hear.'

'Why's Toby at your place?' She still couldn't call it her house. If she did she'd be admitting that she liked sharing a home with Dan and his daughter.

'Sometimes Bea leaves him with us. Leah adores him and wants her own puppy, which I don't have the time for. It would be left on its own too much with me at work and Leah going to kindergarten.' Dan reached for her hand, began walking again.

'Oh.' Why had he taken her hand? *Why* wasn't she tugging it away? 'Dan?' she whispered.

He stopped, turned to her and gently pulled her in against him. His chest was hard and firm under her cheek, his thighs strong against her legs. His hands held her head, each fingertip a touch of magic.

'Sarah.' His voice was low, commanding. Tipping her head back, her breath caught in her throat as Dan's mouth came down to cover hers. Those lips she'd dreamed about for a week now a reality. Only better. Firm, demanding. Was this wise? She pulled away from him. Dan tugged her close again. This time her body folded in against his and she lost herself in the sweet longing his kiss stirred up. His tongue gently probed her mouth, exploring, tasting.

Her arms wound around his back, pulled him even closer. She wanted more of him. She craved all of him.

Lights from a car travelling along the road lit up his face. Toot, toot.

Sarah leapt back, feeling like a guilty schoolgirl. Dan chuckled. 'Takes you back, doesn't it?' He reached for her again. 'But I don't remember kisses being like this.'

Neither did she. Under his mouth her lips curved into a wide smile. Kissing was rapidly becoming her favourite pastime. Her fingers touched the light stubble on his jaw, traced over his bristly cheeks. That quintessential maleness sent shivers of desire down her spine, spreading through her body.

The sea air brushed her arms as Dan's hands slid under her blouse. Goose-bumps lifted on her skin. From the air? Or from the excitement of fingers teasing her nerve endings by tracing circles over her back? Her muscles felt languid. Any moment she'd drop to the sand, her legs unable to hold her up. Dragging her hands down his cheeks, over his chin, throat, she touched his chest, the muscles hard through his shirt.

Dan pulled his mouth from hers, stared into her eyes.

'Sarah Livingston, you're going to the undoing of me.' His voice cracked, his mouth took on a wry expression. 'But I am enjoying the experience.'

'Then hush and kiss me some more.' Sarah took a handful of shirtfront and pulled him closer. Her mouth stifled his laugh.

Hungry lips melded with hungry lips. Hot tongues danced around each other. Dan's hands gripped her buttocks, hugged her against him. Heat roared through her, over her. Desire wound between them, joined them. Sarah had no doubt how this would end if she let it. Which was why she pulled back, tearing her mouth away from Dan's, putting space between their bodies. 'I'm not sure we should be doing this. I'm sorry, I got a bit carried away.'

He didn't say a word, just shoved his hands deep into his jeans pockets, staring at her all the while.

How to tell him she wanted him so much but daren't? Her heart wouldn't take another pounding. *But he's not asking for your heart.* Dan might be thinking about having an affair, and she'd thought that's what she wanted too. But some time over the last week or two, somewhere between the hospital and this house, she'd started feeling strongly for this man. And if she went further then she was going to get very hurt when it all crashed to an end when she headed north again.

Turning back towards the house, she glanced over her shoulder. He was skimming pebbles across the wave tops, his shoulders slouched, his chin on his chest.

Her heart rolled over. She wanted him so much it burned, but she was behaving sensibly by walking away.

Dan heaved another pebble, watched it sink into the cold, black water. Why couldn't he keep his hands to himself? His blasted hormones would be the death of him if he wasn't careful. He should be grateful Sarah had had more self control than him. From the moment her mouth had met his he'd had absolutely none.

The next pebble bit the dust, bouncing along the sand. Sarah had been hurt, was still grappling with getting her life back together. She didn't need to add some randy man with his own problems to the mix. She may have wanted him, and he'd swear she did, but she certainly didn't need him. He was bad for her. She had trust issues.

So did he. He needed to be trusted one hundred and ten per cent. Something Celine had found impossible to do once the miscarriages began taking their toll on her. Being accused of infractions where there hadn't been any had hurt him deep inside. No, Sarah was wise to have walked off.

None of which made him feel any happier with himself. Bending down, he tugged his sandals off his feet, tossed them up the beach. Then he started running along the sand, heading away from the house, going faster and faster, trying to outrun the need for Sarah Livingston that gripped him hard.

'Wake up. Now.' Leah tugged at the pillow, disrupting Sarah's sleep and jerking her head. 'Daddy's taking us to the Pancake Rocks.'

Sarah cracked one eye open. 'Hello, lovely.' Who let little girls out of bed before midday in the weekend?

Leah giggled. 'Hello, sleepy.' Then she began pulling back the sheet. 'Get up. We're having pancakes for breakfast.'

Breakfast? It was far too early. The bedside clock showed eight-thirty. Definitely too early. She tried to retrieve the sheet and a tug of war ensured. Leah won.

'Why pancakes?' Sarah flopped back against her pillow, her stomach groaning at the thought of something so heavy this early.

'Cos we're going to the Pancake Rocks. Get it?'

'Leah, I'm not going there.'

'Daddy said you were.' Leah's bottom lip pushed into a pout, turning Sarah into a spoilsport.

'Sorry, Leah. I'm going to the library today.' She'd decided to join up and get back into reading for pleasure, something she hadn't done for years.

'Daddy will make you come.'

Daddy, whose fault it was she'd been awake for a substantial part of the remainder of the night. 'Your father,' she ground out, 'is making assumptions.'

'Not at all.' A deep, gravelly voice cut across the room from the doorway.

Instinctively Sarah reached for the sheet, pulling it from Leah's grasp, tucking it around her throat. When she looked at Dan he had a glazed look. Because he'd seen her in a negligee? Surely not. Looking around the room, checking out Leah, she couldn't see what else might've put that look on his face.

Dan's tongue slid across his bottom lip. 'Have you ever been to Punakaiki?'

He knew very well she hadn't. 'I must've driven past it on my way here but didn't see anything through the driving rain.'

'Then you're in for an experience.' Dan finally dragged his gaze away from her and looked to his daughter. 'You'd better get dressed, my girl. No one eats pancakes in their pyjamas.'

'Hello? Dan? Which part of "I'm not going" don't you understand? I'm on call, remember? I've also got a patient round to do. There are people expecting to go home today.'

'All taken care of.'

That was it? All taken care of? She rolled one hand through the air, finishing palm up pointing at him. 'How? Who? Since when did you think you can organise my life? My work?'

'By phone, Charlie, this morning.' His smile was slow and cheeky, and devastating to her heart. 'You are entitled to weekends off, you know.'

Dan whisked the pancake batter fast. He wanted sex so badly he hurt. Not just any old sex either. Only the kind that involved Sarah Livingston.

She looked beautiful in that black negligee thing, the front scooping down over the swell of her breasts. He didn't get why she wore those things when she went to bed alone. What a waste. But she had come out of a relationship so maybe she had drawers full of the stuff. His teeth were grinding hard.

'Look, Daddy, Sarah helped me get dressed.'

Dan peered down at his daughter, the familiar tug of love tightening his gut. 'You look pretty, little one.' How had Sarah managed to cajole Leah into wearing that particular T-shirt with those cute shorts? He'd never been able to persuade Leah that the elephant on the shirt was not going to squash the puppies on the shorts. A tick for Sarah.

'Are the pancakes ready?' Leah dragged a chair over to the bench and hopped up to take the bowl from his hands. 'Can I stir them? You didn't put blueberries in them. How many are you making? I don't know if Sarah likes pancakes. She didn't say.' Leah turned towards the door. 'Sarah. Do you like pancakes?' she yelled at the top of her lungs.

Dan covered his ears and grinned at his girl. 'You'll wake the seagulls with that racket.'

Leah giggled. 'Daddy, they are already up. There're lots of them. Look out the window.'

He did, and noted the birds circling a spot on the beach. A dead fish or bird must've washed up on the morning tide. 'We'll go and take a look while we wait for slowcoach.'

'Who's a slowcoach?' Sarah stood in the doorway, dressed in perfectly fitting, white knee-length shorts and a crimson, thin-strapped top that hugged her curves.

And sent his pulse rate into orbit. He turned away to break the connection he felt with her. Otherwise he'd reach out to take her into his arms and kiss her senseless. Despite the talking to he'd given himself on the beach last night. 'Why don't you two go and see what the gulls are squawking about while I make these pancakes? But don't take too long.' Just long enough for him collect his scattered emotions.

Idiot. That would take for ever. He tapped his forehead. You invited, actually insisted, that Sarah come with us today. Now you're going to spend the whole day noticing how sexy she is every time you look at her. Idiot, he repeated.

Through the window he saw Sarah take Leah's hand as they got close to the road. Sarah had the right instincts with his child, for sure. And Leah liked her.

So did he. A lot. This wasn't about lust. Some time while he'd been trying to keep her at bay she'd sneaked in under his skin anyway. Touched his heart and had him wanting to share so much more with her. Truth? From the moment he'd set eyes on her he'd felt a connection that would take more than a tumble in the sheets to fix.

But last night had shown she wasn't ready. And neither was he.

He dropped a large knob of butter into the hot pan and poured in some batter. The smell of melted butter teased his senses, overlaying the scent of Sarah that permeated the house these days. She'd made her presence felt in a lot of little ways. Like those stinky lilies on the dining table. At least the roses she'd bought yesterday smelt sweet. Even if she'd only put something back in its place at a different angle, he felt her aura. In every room except his bedroom.

He hadn't felt this much in need of intimacy in for ever. If this was what stopping work for a while did then he should be getting back to the job. Except that his former life, that one prior to the arrival of Sarah, now seemed dull and uninteresting.

He flipped the first pancake. He needed a hobby. Tomorrow was supposed to be fine. He'd put the surf-board in the water, try riding a wave or two, and likely make a fool of himself. Anything would be better then hanging around Sarah like a lovelorn teen.

'Those pancakes were fabulous.' Sarah stacked dishes in the sink and began wiping down the table. 'Now, off you go and enjoy the rocky version.'

Dan put his hand over hers, effectively stopping the wiping. 'Please come with us. I'd really like you to.'

Spending a day in Dan's company without the benefit of staff or his family to break the friction between them would only increase the tension. 'Leah needs more time with you, just you.'

'She doesn't need my attention every single minute of the day. Now, I…' he tapped his muscular chest '…need some adult company.' His finger under her chin tilted her head back. His eyes met hers, pleading with her. 'Please say you'll come.'

'I shouldn't.'

'Why ever not?' He turned them both to look out the

window. 'How many stunning, clear days like this one have you seen since you arrived?'

'We had one yesterday.' A trip out would be fun, a day away from patients and staff and decisions. She'd been here nearly a month and because of Dan she now had her first full day off. The library was never going to compete.

'I've packed lunch for when we're watching the water spouts and the seals. I used your salmon steak to make a quiche and there're plenty of salads left over from last night.'

'Okay,' she submitted, and felt surprisingly relaxed about it. Suddenly it seemed like time to go and play.

'Daddy, what are those animals? The ones on the pancakes?'

Dan sat Leah on the rail of the safety fence circling the top of the viewing platform and held her firmly. 'Those are seals. They're sunbathing after hunting fish in the sea.'

'I want to pat one.'

'Definitely not, my girl. Seals give big, nasty bites.' Loud grunts could be heard over the waves crashing against the edge of the Punakaiki Rocks. 'Listen to them talking. They sound like you with a tummyache.'

'Do not.'

Sarah studied the cumbersome brown bodies sprawled across the sun-warmed rocks. 'Hard to believe how fast they can move, isn't it?'

'I've seen a grown man running pretty quick with a seal snapping at his heels.' Dan grinned. 'It was funny once the guy made it to safety. We ribbed him about it for weeks.'

'Charming.' Sarah heard the tide roaring in. 'Look at the pancakes, Leah. You might see the water fountain coming out the top.'

'Where? I can't see, Sarah. Show me.'

Sarah leaned on the railing, putting her head close to Leah's, and pointed. 'See that rock that looks a bit like Dad's stack of pancakes? They're a lot bigger than your father's and not as lopsided.' Sweet little-girl smell teased her, made her want to cuddle Leah. 'The rocks on the other side of the seal that's staring at you?'

She stood up straight again. Warm masculine smell tantalised her. Since when did men smell so divine? Or was Dan the only one who did?

'I can't see the fountain.'

'Patience, my girl.' Dan jiggled Leah, smiling over the top of her head at Sarah, sending Sarah's heart rate into overdrive. 'Lopsided, huh?'

'The maple syrup only ran one way.' She grinned at him, her heart turning over. 'Your way.' He looked magnificent in his navy chinos and white shirt so new she'd had to cut the label off the collar as they'd made their way out of the house earlier.

He looked so relaxed and comfortable that Sarah wondered why she'd argued about coming. She couldn't remember the last time she'd enjoyed herself so much. And there wasn't a spa or upmarket wine bar in sight. Three people happy to be together doing something as simple as having a picnic and staring at blowholes in the rocks. Like a real family. Everything seemed easy here with Dan. All the usual worries and fears that haunted her had disappeared in the magic of the day.

She said, 'You never mention your parents.' Neither did she, come to think of it.

Dan looked at her over the top of Leah's head. Sadness tinged the piercing blue of his eyes. 'Mum died of cancer six years ago. Dad missed her so much he died of a broken heart a year later.'

'I'm sorry, that must've hurt.'

'It did. We all felt we might've let Dad down. But at the same time they'd had such a strong marriage I can see why one couldn't live without the other.'

'That's lovely, I think,' Sarah sighed. 'You know, I sometimes wonder about my parents. When Bobby died they separated, but neither of them has remarried, or even had a deep and meaningful relationship.' Her father had found solace in his work.

'You're wondering if they still love each other?'

'I'm being silly. They can't, not after the horrible things they said to each other back then.' But stress did funny things to people. 'I know Dad still supports my mother in a very lavish way, bought her a beautiful house in an up-market suburb, makes sure she has support in anything she does.'

Dan turned to her. 'You always say Dad and my mother, not Mum. Are you not close to your mother?'

Her lips pressed together for a moment. 'I guess not. We never seemed to have anything in common.'

'I'm hungry.' Leah twisted around in her father's arms. 'Can we have our picnic?'

Dan laughed. 'You've only just had breakfast. We'll go for a walk first.'

An hour later Sarah spread a blanket on a patch of grass where they could overlook the rocks and Dan unpacked the lunch he'd put together. Leah sipped a juice and leapt around laughing and talking nonstop.

'I wish I had as much energy.' Sarah leaned on an elbow, her legs stretched out over the grass.

Dan's gaze landed on Sarah. 'Glad you came?'

'Actually, yes. It's ages since I've been on a picnic.' When had the last time been? 'I remember Gran taking my brother and me to the beach once.'

'Only once?' Dan didn't bother to hide his surprise.

'Now I think about it, she took me a few times.' How had she forgotten those happier times? Well, whatever was in the water down here it had given her memory a tickle.

'Did she always take your brother as well?'

Behind her eyes she could see Bobby sitting on the red plaid blanket. She could feel the childish jealousy that used to flare up within her. She'd wanted Gran all to herself. 'Gran was the only adult in our family who gave equal attention to both of us. I latched onto that as my parents were so busy I missed out on a fair bit.'

'Because you were the youngest? Or because they were too busy with their careers?'

'Mum gave up work when she married and had Bobby. Dad was definitely into establishing himself in the surgical field. Add in conferences, studying and teaching. All those things kept him very busy.' But he did come home for Bobby. It wasn't until later that he'd stopped coming home at night.

Dan touched the back of her hand with a finger. 'And you missed him?'

Sarah bit the inside of her cheek. Turned her hand over and wound her fingers through Dan's, drawing warmth from his touch. 'All the time. I tried everything to get his attention, from being super-good to being a teenage brat. I'm not proud of that.' That hadn't got her anywhere either. By then her brother had become severely ill, and he'd got most of their parents' time.

'I imagine you were only doing what any kid would do in the circumstances. I don't know what you did but I'm sure I'd have been ten times worse.' He paused, staring over Punakaiki. 'I wonder.'

'Yes?'

'Is that what I've done to Leah? I know I haven't been

there very much for her, always busy at work. What if she doesn't even know how much I love her?'

'Dan, your love shows in everything you do.' Had her own dad always loved her? Did he now? He'd sent her here, hadn't he? He'd seen she wasn't coping after Oliver had dumped her. Wasn't that love? She wasn't sure. Her father equally could've been putting the clinic first as an overworked surgeon could become a liability.

Beside her Dan said, 'I hope you're right.'

'You've taken three months off for her. I'd have given anything for my father to do that.' She nibbled her lip. 'I followed him into surgery partly so I could work with him.'

'Daddy, I want a biscuit.'

'Can I have a biscuit, please,' Dan gently admonished his daughter. 'And, no, not until you've had a sandwich.' Then he squeezed Sarah's hand and dropped a light kiss on her cheek. 'Ready for some food?'

She stared into his eyes, looking for pity, found only understanding. Her shoulders lifted, her mouth curved into a smile. 'I'm starving.'

Dan drove carefully, his two passengers sound asleep after their day out. They'd all had so much fun. Once Sarah had got over her hesitation about joining them she'd made the day really work, giving a sparkle to everything they'd done.

Leah clearly adored her. Today she'd seemed even happier than usual, getting all the attention she needed from him and Sarah. Like they were a real family. Unlike what Sarah had grown up with. She wouldn't know a lot about children, and yet she always seemed to get it right with Leah. Did Sarah want kids?

His hands tightened on the steering-wheel. Why did any of this concern him? His feelings for Sarah had little to do with families, more to do with raging hormones and hot sex. Didn't it? Even if he had started developing deeper feelings for her he wasn't ready to contemplate going down the relationship track. He'd believed he'd had the perfect marriage with Celine and that had gone pear-shaped when the depression had come into their lives.

'What's that grim look for?' Sarah's voice was sleepy. She stretched her legs as much as the cramped confines of the vehicle allowed. 'I thought you'd enjoyed your day.'

'I've had a wonderful day, thanks to you.' Dan's eyes slid sideways to gawp at her knees. He quickly turned his attention back to the road. But his tongue cleaved to the roof of his mouth. See? This whole Sarah thing was about sex, and only sex. If they didn't make it into bed soon he would explode, and if they did hit the sack they'd open up a whole new can of problems.

And then his mouth got the better of him. 'Since it's your day off, let's make the most of it and go out for dinner tonight. I'm sure Jill or Bea will take Leah for the evening.'

He shot a quick glance over at his disturbing passenger, saw her tongue do a fast circuit of her lips. Should've kept his eyes on the road. Too late. Even now that he'd refocused on the tarmac unfolding before his vehicle he couldn't get the sight of her tongue out of his befuddled brain. What was happening to him? He'd agreed with himself that he had to put space between them, give her time, and then he'd gone and asked her out. On a date. Dinner for two. No child involved.

It's all right. She'll say no, for sure.

'I'd like that.'

So, he knew absolutely nothing about women. Especially this one.

CHAPTER NINE

DAN placed his elbows on the table and laid his chin on his interlaced fingers, his gaze fixed on Sarah. 'How was your venison?'

'Divine.' Instantly she wished she hadn't licked her lips as Dan's eyes followed her tongue. Pushing her plate aside, she struggled to come up with a conversation starter that would divert his attention. 'Leah had a great time today.' How lame was that?

'She'll drive Jill mad talking about it until she goes to bed.'

Bed. Dan. Funny how the two words seemed to combine in her head. She really had it bad for him. 'Today was wonderfully exciting for her.' And me.

Mischief twinkled in Dan's eyes. 'I'm discovering I like doing exciting things. Coming out for dinner falls into that category. It's been so long since I did anything remotely like it.'

Was it the dinner that was exciting? Not her company? She'd had a lot of dinners, and most of them at far more sophisticated restaurants than this one, but she couldn't remember feeling quite so relaxed and tense at the same time in any of them. 'You should make a regular thing of eating out.'

Dan nodded, then asked, 'What's it like, working with

the famous Dr David Livingston? I remember hearing a
lot about him when I was training.'

Sarah sank down into her chair. 'He's a hard taskmaster.
You give your absolute best and it's never good enough.
And that's not just with me, he treats all his staff the same.'

'Bet he gets the results, though.'

'Yes, everyone strives to impress him.' They all wanted
his attention in one way or another. That could be hard on
her father at times.

'But you haven't followed his penchant for research.'

'I considered it, but no.' Her fingers fidgeted with the
dessert spoon lying on the table.

'Not interested?' Dan's question seemed innocuous
enough, but would he understand how much pain was behind her reply?

'Not really.'

'I'd have thought that would've been the way to get the
attention you craved.' His fingers lightly brushed the back
of her hand.

So he did understand. 'So did I, but I quickly found it
didn't suit me. I enjoyed fixing people, using tried and true
techniques.'

Dan was studying her closely. 'Enjoyed? As in the past?
Not any more?' He didn't miss a thing.

'I had begun losing interest in surgery. For every operation we did, two more people popped up on the list and
I began to feel I was working by rote.' She glanced into
those blue eyes, saw understanding. 'I always did the absolute best I could. But before I came down here I'd reached
the stage where there seemed to be so many patients that
if one walked up to me in the street the day after I'd operated on them I'd not have known who they were. That
doesn't seem right to me, doesn't seem to be the reason I

started on this career in the first place. I felt I'd lost my compassion, my need to heal.'

'Sounds familiar,' Dan drawled. 'We have something in common. We were both sent away from our jobs to get some perspective.'

A small smile tugged at her mouth. 'And it is working for both of us. You're getting your life back, discovering the joys of those big toys you'd hidden away in your shed, having fun with your daughter. I'm finding the fun in surgery again. It's great to work with other professionals who are there for the good of the locals and the hospital, not arguing amongst themselves over who's the best. I'm finding I enjoy operating on people that I'm likely to bump into again.' Her smile widened. 'Two days ago I walked into the supermarket and little Emma Duncan came charging down one of the aisles calling out to Dr Sarah and landing a big kiss on my chin. At least it would have been my chin if she'd been a metre taller.' It had felt so good.

Dan laughed. 'There you go. You're fitting right in here.'

Which reminded her... 'Charlie talked to me yesterday. About staying on at the end of my contract.'

Blue eyes bored into hers, the smile hovering on Dan's lips frozen. 'What did you say?'

'That I'd think about it.' Which was a giant step forward considering she'd arrived here intent on getting through the three months and hightailing it back to Auckland quick smart. 'There are a lot of things to consider, not least my father and his clinic.'

'How will he feel if you sell your partnership?'

Once she'd have said he'd be disappointed, angry even, but now she could see how he'd been trying to help her by sending her away. 'Maybe he'd be happy for me.' Sarah leaned forward, watching Dan closely as she asked, 'But how would you feel if I did stay on? It is your clinic. You've built it up from scratch. Do you want someone working alongside you? Specifically, do you want me in that role?'

Caution filtered through the blue, making his eyes dark and brooding. 'If I say I don't know the answer to any of those questions, you've got to understand I'm not trying to hurt you.'

She dipped her head in acknowledgment, hoping he didn't see the spurt of disappointment she'd felt. 'Sure.'

'I'm surprised Charlie has approached you so soon. I thought he'd wait until the end of March, and I admit I was putting off making up my mind about the hours I want to work until then, too. But one thing's certain, I'm not going back to working those long hours I did before I got kicked off the roster. Not when I'm finally straightening out things at home.'

'You were hardly kicked off.'

'Of course I was, and fair enough. I needed to be.' Dan glanced out the window, back to her. 'I guess the only question I can't really give you an answer to is do I want you to stay on? There's a lot more to that question than hospital hours. It's early days to be contemplating that.'

Her stomach tightened uncomfortably. Her heart squeezed and slowed. 'I shouldn't have asked.'

'Always tell me what's on your mind. That's being honest.' His hand touched hers again, covered it, holding her fingers in his. A caress that quickly went from warm to heated.

She certainly wasn't telling him what was on her mind right this instant. It had nothing to do with clinics and hours and staying or going. All to do with desire and hunger and need. All to do with learning more about each other, taking this thing between them to another level, admitting what she'd been denying since the day she'd arrived in town. Daniel Reilly was hot and she wanted him. Come what may.

Tugging her hand away, she swallowed around the heat blocking her throat. 'Can we order some coffee?'

'In a hurry to get home?'

She'd ride a speeding bullet to get there. 'No, definitely not.'

His eyes now sparkling with heat, Dan said, slowly teasing out the words, 'We've got the whole night to enjoy.' Sexual tension ricocheted between them.

Was that a promise? Her blood cranked up its pace, racing through her veins. Was she finally going to touch those muscles, feel all that hard body, kiss that suntanned skin? What had happened to her usual arguments for keeping distant from Dan? He wanted her to be honest with him. Right now she was being honest with herself. She wanted him.

'Let's have dessert.' Dan leaned over the table, his mouth barely moving, the tip of his tongue slipping across his bottom lip.

She'd never manage to swallow a dot. Her stomach was wound so tight it would repel food like a tennis racquet hitting a ball. She squeaked, 'I'll have the cheesecake.'

He smiled, a long, lazy smile that curled her toes and tightened her belly. 'How do you know they've got cheesecake?'

Thankfully their waitress appeared. 'Would you like to see the dessert menu?'

Dan leaned back and looked up at the girl. 'Have you got cheesecake?'

'Boysenberry or lemon,' she replied.

Dan lifted an eyebrow at Sarah in a quirky fashion, making her incapable of deciding which flavour to have. Not that it mattered, if eating was beyond her.

'Lemon,' she croaked.

'Make mine berry,' Dan told the girl as he reached for his glass of water and took a long drink.

The desserts seemed to arrive in super-quick time as though the staff were working at keeping her wound tight.

Dan picked up his spoon and dipped into the cheese-cake. His mouth closed over the spoon, and he slowly slid it out over those lips she ached to kiss. 'Divine,' he whispered. 'You should try it.'

Just like that the delicious tension rippled through her body, sending out tingles of desire so sharp her fingers shook. She pushed her plate aside. Her appetite had totally disappeared. For dessert, that was. Not for Dan. Dan she wanted to kiss and taste and—

He stood up abruptly and came around the table. 'Let's get out of here.'

'Did you pay the bill?' she asked ten minutes later as Dan swung into their drive.

'I think so.' Dan slammed to a stop at the back door. He was out of the Land Cruiser and around at her door so fast he had to be dizzy.

She practically fell out, into his arms. His hands gripping her shoulders were hot on her suddenly hyper-sensitive skin.

His eyes locked with hers. The baby blue caution was gone, replaced with such carnal intensity that she rocked back on her heels. Her lungs stalled. Without any order from her mind her hands gripped the front of his shirt, tugged him closer. Then her lips sought his, found them, covered them. She gave herself up to kissing him. Heady kisses that he returned enthusiastically.

His tongue pushed between her lips, tangled with hers. He tasted wonderful. Hot male. From deep inside a groan crawled up her throat, giving sound to a primitive longing. A need to make love, a hungry urge to be with this man intimately.

Then his hands were pressing her shoulders away from him. 'Sarah, I've wanted to touch you all day.' His voice caught in his throat. 'If we take this any further, I won't guarantee I can stop.'

Leaning back, she looked into those beguiling eyes again. 'I won't ask you to. I don't want you to.'

'You're sure?' His hands held her face, his thumbs rubbing exquisitely tender circles across her cheek bones.

Sarah nodded, unable to speak around the need blocking her throat. She was past being able to hold out. Past rationalising. She wanted him.

'Then why are we standing out here?' Dan took her hand in his and together they raced for the house.

Inside he leaned back against the door and pulled her close again. His mouth found hers, his tongue slid between her lips. Pent-up desire exploded through her taut body. Heat, molten fire, spread through her muscles, her stomach. Her bones liquefied, no longer able to hold her up. Dan alone did that. He wound her tight against him. His response pressed hard against her belly.

Her tongue explored his mouth. Tasted him. She fell against him, needing to touch the whole length of his body with hers. It wasn't enough. Her hands ran over his back, down to his buttocks, over the curves. She was touching those muscles she'd been sneaking looks at for days. Weeks.

Clothing lay between her and his skin. She tried to slide her hands under the waist of his trousers. They were a tight fit. Frustration made her groan, and her mouth temporarily slid away from his.

Dan pulled his mouth well clear. 'This dress...' he slid the thin straps off her shoulders and down to her elbows

'…is stunning but it has to go.' His head ducked and he ran feather-light kisses down her neck, further down between her breasts. His hands gently pushed her dress further and further down, over her breasts, past her stomach, the hemline lowering from mid-thigh to her knees, pooling at her ankles. The silk fabric light and sensual against her skin, Dan's lips hot and demanding as they trailed a line of kisses from her breasts to her stomach. And lower.

She ached to touch him. Everywhere. Her hands touched here, there. Hard to concentrate while he stroked her. Would Dan be shocked if he knew how desperate she was to take him inside her? Her eyes flew open, met his delirious gaze. No, he wouldn't. The bite she gave her bottom lip stung, sharpening all her senses. Who was this woman acting wantonly?

Dan smiled, a quick curling of those full lips that made her heart flip. 'Bedroom. Now.'

She'd never remember how they got from the back door to Dan's bedroom. She only remembered falling onto the soft, cool bed, Dan sprawling on top of her. His tongue traced a hot, slick path over her taut nipple, moving around, over, beneath, until she believed her skin would split wide with desire. He was merciless, and she cried out for more. The only reprieve came when he swapped one nipple for the other and began again. Between her legs the heat built into a hot, moist pool, reaching an intensity she'd never experienced, never believed possible. How much more could she take? How long would this last before she fell apart in his hands?

'Dan, I can't wait. Can we…?' Then she blushed.

He grinned, a wicked, heated grin that did nothing to slow the rapid pounding of her heart. 'We need some protection, if I've got any.' Horror showed in his eyes.

She managed a chuckle. 'All sorted.' Pregnancy was one thing she'd never risk.

'Thank goodness. For a moment there I thought I'd have to do the impossible and stop.'

Her hands hooked at the back of his head, caught at his hair. 'Oh—my—Dan.' She didn't recognise her voice. It was raspy, fragmented.

And then at last they were together as one. Sarah's world exploded into a trillion beautiful fragments as Dan tipped her over the edge into that place where there was no beginning and no end, only pleasure and fulfilment. And so much more.

'You can remove the padding from Toby's throat.' Sarah nodded at Jill over the prostate body of their patient.

Jill used surgical tongs to lift the blood-soaked cotton padding that had been used to prevent blood pouring down the boy's throat during the tonsillectomy. While Sarah waited she arched her back, turned her head left then right, freeing the tight muscles of her neck.

'It's been a long day,' Hamish stood up from his seat at Toby's head, leaned over his monitors to begin bringing his patient round.

Sarah swallowed a yawn. 'It sure has, and we're not finished.' They'd started the day with a breast lumpectomy, followed by a torn Achilles' tendon.

'Anyone for coffee before the next one?' Jill asked.

'Most definitely. An extra-strong one for me.' She needed a caffeine fix. Too much late-night activity at home had left her happily tired. Since dinner on Saturday her relationship with Dan had ramped up big time. It had begun raining on Sunday, continued through Monday, Tuesday, Wednesday, making him restless. Until night-time after

Leah was sound asleep and then he came to life. They'd fall
into his bed, making love as though they'd just invented it.

She was astonished at her appetite for Dan. Occasionally
she'd lie awake beside his warm body and wonder where
they went from there. It frightened her to think that she
wanted more, was beginning to seriously considering staying on in Port Weston—if Dan agreed to the idea. During
the early evenings when Sarah couldn't go for her usual
after-work walk they'd talked and talked about just about
everything. But not about what would happen come the
end of March.

Neither had Sarah told him about the CF gene she carried. If they were going to take their relationship any further, she had to tell him. The day would arrive when she
had to ask him to take the test to see if he was a carrier too.
If he was, there'd be some huge decisions to make about
taking the chance on having a baby that might have cystic
fibrosis. One thing at a time, she told herself.

'What was that noise?' Hamish asked the room in general.

'Sarah's stomach,' Jill replied.

'A chocolate biscuit wouldn't go amiss,' Sarah agreed.

'We didn't have chocolate biscuits until you arrived.'
Hamish grinned.

'I'm not that bad.' They didn't have them at the clinic
back home either. Everyone there watched waistlines more
carefully than the six-o'clock news.

'Yes, you are,' Jill and Hamish answered in unison.

A girl had to keep her energy levels up. Sarah's vinyl
gloves snapped as she tugged them off, and she idly wondered what Dan had been doing during the day. He'd hoped
to go fishing with mates but while the rain had lightened
a strong wind had picked up. Just thinking about the man
made her warm.

'What's that smile about?' Jill murmured quietly as she cleared away dirty instruments and blood soaked cotton. 'Or should I say who?'

'Nosey, nosey.' Sarah elbowed her way through the doors and began to change out of her theatre scrubs.

'You've had a permanent grin on your face for the last three days. What have you two been up to?' Jill was right behind her.

'I'm a smiley person.' Especially after mind-blowing sex before coming to work.

Jill rolled her eyes. 'Whatever you say.'

Familiar male laughter came from the other side of the door. Sarah gaped as Dan sauntered through dressed in scrubs and talking with the house surgeon. Her heart rate raced, her fingers itched to touch him.

'Anyone want one?' He said.

'Where's Leah?' Sarah asked.

'Hello to you, too.' Dan shot her a quick, secret look. 'She's gone to the movies with Bea and the girls.'

'But why have you come in here?' She leaned closer and whispered, 'I haven't got time to sneak into the linen cupboard with you.'

A huge sigh crossed his lips. 'Damn. I had such high hopes.' He suddenly looked serious. 'There was an accident on one of the fishing boats a couple of hours ago. A winch handle snapped and smashed into one of the men, rupturing his liver. Since you were already busy with a big schedule, I put my hand up to help out.'

She'd have liked to watch Dan at work. As opposed to watching him in the kitchen, the garden, the bedroom. 'I hope you don't think this excuses you from cooking dinner. It's your turn.'

'On my way to the supermarket as soon as I've finished this.' He waved his mug through the air. 'Bossy woman.'

Sarah chuckled. 'Someone's got to be.'

Jill's jaw dropped, and she looked from Sarah to Dan and back again.

'What?' Sarah asked.

Jill shook her head. 'He's laughing and joking. Whatever you've done to him, keep it up.'

Sarah spluttered into her coffee. 'Time we went back to work. Mabel Carpenter's hernia is next, isn't it?'

Sarah watched Robert closely as he brought across the coffee she'd ordered. His limp was very pronounced, putting his posture out of alignment and no doubt making his hips ache. Fatigue darkened his eyes and lined his mouth. Why did he put up with it?

George caught her eye and shrugged. 'I keep trying,' he said quietly.

But not quietly enough.

'What do you keep trying?' Robert asked, placing the large cups on the table.

'To get you to see another doctor about that leg,' George said.

Robert scowled at him. 'Don't waste your breath. I'm never going through all that again.'

George ignored the outburst, turning instead to Sarah. 'See what I have to put up with, cupcakes?'

Sarah was torn between smiling at her new name and taking Robert's fear seriously. Cupcakes won—for a moment. And then it was too late to talk to Robert as a customer came in, demanding coffee strong enough to take the soles off his shoes.

George raised an eyebrow. 'We sure get them.' Then he leaned closer to Sarah. 'Could you talk to him? He's in a bad way. He thinks I don't know how often he gets up at night because of the pain, but I'm aware the instant he gets out of bed.'

'I'll do my best.' But Sarah knew that would be woefully little unless Robert wanted to talk with her.

Then a familiar voice called across the room, 'Morning, guys. Is that my coffee? Or are you having two, Sarah?'

'I don't want coffee, Daddy.' Leah bounded over to George. 'Can I have a juice?'

'Please,' Dan told her.

'Please, George, can I?'

'Come with me, young lady. I'm sure there's a special treat somewhere for you to go with that juice.'

Watching Leah slip her hand into George's and skip along beside him Sarah felt the now familiar tug at her heart. So much for not getting involved with the child. Or her father. She was more than halfway in love with the guy. Leaving was rapidly becoming the last thing she wanted to do.

'Sarah?' Dan grinned down at her. 'I've bought you a present.'

She studied the large plastic bag with a local farmer's supply shop logo that he placed in front of her. Squinting up at him, she asked, 'What have you done?'

'Just a little number for your shoe collection.'

'Gumboots?' She dug into the bag and pulled out bright red boots painted with sunflowers. 'Heck, I don't think I've seen anything quite like them.' She jumped up and kissed Dan's cheek. 'They're gorgeous.'

He looked smug. 'Thought they'd come in handy now that you've turned into a gardener.'

Sarah slipped her sandals off and slid her feet into the gumboots. They fitted perfectly. When she raised an eyebrow at Dan he told her, 'I borrowed a pair of your shoes to take with me.'

'They are absolutely perfect in all ways.'

'I thought so.' His phone buzzed with an incoming text. 'Excuse me.'

Sarah dropped back onto her chair, staring at the red and yellow creations on her feet. Laughter bubbled up her throat. Laughing at herself. She was changing so much. Gumboots. They'd look way out of place back in her apartment. Face it, there wasn't any gardening to do there either. Over the week she'd started tidying up the vegetable patch that had gone to weeds. She planted seedlings for salads and soups later in the year. Most of them she wouldn't be here to pick unless… She looked at Dan, love pulsing through her. Unless she committed to staying. Her laughter died.

Did she know Dan well enough to take the risk? How would he react if she said yes to Charlie? Did he expect her to consult further with him about that first? When she'd mentioned it the other night he'd said they needed more time. He needed more time. She didn't. She was ready to stay.

But if Dan wasn't ready for that then maybe he wouldn't be ready to face the cystic-fibrosis issue either. And she definitely couldn't cope again with the dillydallying about having that test done. Oliver had become a dab hand at putting it off every time she'd raised the subject. He'd assured her he could deal with the consequences, whatever they were, but as time had gone by and he hadn't spoken to his GP, she'd had to question that. Oliver had blamed her, saying if she left him alone he'd have done it months earlier. Said if she hadn't nagged him he wouldn't have turned to someone else for comfort. Yeah, right.

Now she wondered if he'd been afraid of learning he wasn't perfect. That would rock him, big time. His image was important to him, his ego huge. Something like being a gene carrier would punch a hole in that ego. And a sweet little obliging nurse wouldn't question his perfection.

Dan had intimated he'd had problems with Celine, although he'd never elaborated to her what they had been. Problems he only now seemed to be coming to terms with. Could she ask him to deal with hers so soon? How would he respond if she asked him to take a test for the gene? Probably very well. He was an empathetic man.

Was she willing to test how compassionate Dan really was? There was a risk he'd walk away from the whole issue, walk away from her. She shuddered. Like Oliver had done before him.

CHAPTER TEN

'WE'RE going horse riding,' Dan told Sarah on Saturday morning. 'Bea wants to give the horses a bit of a workout. Want to come with us? We could tell the hospital where you are in case you're needed.'

Sarah glanced out the window. The rain had finally played ball and disappeared, leaving a sparkling day. 'As long as I don't have to mount a horse, I'm all for it.'

Unfortunately Dan appeared to have selective hearing. Bea had three horses waiting when they pulled into the yard.

'Look, Sarah, there's Flicker and Jumbo and Sammy.' Leah's arm shot in front of Sarah's face, her little finger pointing to the massive animals.

Sarah gulped. 'Bea going with you?'

Dan climbed out of the Land Cruiser and slapped a hat on. 'Not that I know of.'

Another gulp. 'You haven't got me out here under false pretences, have you, Daniel Reilly?'

'I never said you wouldn't be riding. You did. It's my job to change your mind.'

'Not this side of Christmas, you're not.' Sarah stayed in the vehicle, staring through the window at the big beasts, their backs a long way from the ground. 'I'll wait here for you. In case the hospital phones.' Her knuckles were white in her lap.

Leah had already climbed the fence and was petting one of the horses. 'I presume that's Flicker.' Leah looked so tiny beside the horse. How could Dan even consider letting the child ride it? 'Don't you worry about Leah getting thrown off?'

'Yes, which is why someone always goes with her.' Dan stood at the door, his hand on her shoulder. 'Sammy's the smallest of the other two, if you change your mind.'

'He's enormous. My feet won't be anywhere near the ground.' Her heart was racing.

'You're confusing this with the merry-go-round.' Dan leaned in to give her a kiss. 'At least come over with me to give Leah a leg up. We can walk around the paddock with her.'

Bea came out from the house, surrounded by children, some of whom Sarah recognised as Dan's nieces and others she'd never seen before. 'Crikey,' Sarah muttered, beginning to feel inundated as they all crowded around.

Dan laughed. 'It's always like this out here. Bea's kids have a lot of friends and half the reason for that is Bea is so good with them.'

'Hi, there.' Bea waved over the many heads. 'What do you think, Sarah? Want to have a go? Sammy's so quiet you'll struggle to get him moving.'

'No, thanks, I'm into spectator sports.' Wimp. Sarah moved closer to Dan. When he took her hand she hoped he wouldn't notice how much she shook. 'I don't mind going up and patting horses, but that's as far I go.'

'Fair enough.' Dan grinned and slapped her bottom lightly. In front of his sister?

Who, when Sarah glanced at her, had definitely noticed the gesture and was smiling at them both. Great. Why were Bea and Jill so keen for Dan to get friendly with her? Hadn't they read the bit in the contract that said she was only here for three months? Did they want to see him get hurt again?

Everyone, including Sarah, climbed the fence to join Leah. Dan hoisted Leah up into the saddle, helped her slide her feet into the stirrups.

Sarah marvelled at Leah's poise. 'Like a pro.'

Bea agreed. 'Born to it, I reckon, same as with all my kids.'

Dan mounted and followed Leah around the paddock. Sarah couldn't take her eyes off him. Sitting straight and tall, his hands firm yet relaxed on the reins, his thighs pressing the horse's flanks, it was a sight she'd never forget. Simply beautiful.

'Have you ever ridden?' Bea's question scratched against the image holding Sarah enthralled.

'Once. The ride lasted all of three minutes before I was unceremoniously tossed off over the horse's head and into a blackberry bush. Definitely not my thing. Trust me on this.'

Bea smiled in sympathy. 'I can see how that could put you off. But who knows, one day we might get you in a saddle again.'

'What is it with the Reillys that none of you will take no for an answer?' Sarah smiled to take the sting out of her words.

'Guess we only see things from our point of view, and because we know how much fun riding is we want to share it with you.'

'How about I take your word for it?'

Dan trotted over to them. 'Want to try?' he asked Sarah. 'Trust me. I won't let anything happen to you.'

'No, thanks.' Why did he look at her as though she'd

hurt him? Of course she trusted him to look out for her, but so what? It wasn't as though riding a horse was the be-all and end-all.

Dan shrugged stiffly. 'Okay.'

She watched him trot back to Leah. They looked good riding together. Family. But it was only half a picture. There should be a wife, a mother, with them. She was sure she could be there, if she learned to trust again. But she'd sensed over the past week there was something Dan was holding back from her and until he told her, how could she trust him?

'Come and have a coffee,' Bea nudged her. 'Dan and Leah will be a while. The rest of the kids are going eeling and I'd love some adult female chat. At the moment all anyone around here wants to talk about is the camping trip we've got planned for next week.'

'I think you're just being kind, but coffee would be great.' Even an instant one. Which went to show how much she'd changed.

The hours flew past. After the horses had been wiped down and put out to graze Bea put on a simple lunch for everyone, including all the extra kids. John arrived home from the mine where he drove a front-end loader, in time to have a beer with Dan before they ate.

Sarah helped set out the food on a huge outdoor table, watching Bea handle the kids with an ease that made her envious.

'Families, eh? Aren't they great?' She hadn't noticed Dan coming up beside her. Her usual radar had failed. Even the scent of his aftershave was absent today, overlaid with the tang of horse smell.

'Yours seems to have it all worked out. Everyone gets along so well.' Even the children helped each other, despite bickering occasionally.

Dan placed his arm around her shoulders. 'You could still have all this. With the right man.'

Turning, she looked up at him. With you? Was he offering her something she daren't hope for? Did she want to spend the rest of her life with him? Yes, darn it, she did. She loved him. Then start by being honest with him. 'There's something I haven't told you.'

His hand traced a line down her cheek, rested on her chin. 'Go ahead. Fill me in on Sarah Livingston and what makes her tick.'

She pulled away from his warm, heavy arm, took a few steps into the paddock. Stopped. Clenched her hands in front of her, and spun around. 'My brother died of cystic fibrosis. I carry the gene too.'

Three long strides and Dan was before her, taking her cold hands in his. 'Sweetheart, I'm so sorry. Now I begin to understand some of the things I felt you left out when talking about your family.'

'You did?' Was there nothing this man couldn't get right with her?

'Yep.' His hand brushed her hair off her face. 'Thank you for telling me.'

Did he get it? Understand he'd have to be tested for the gene if they were taking this relationship to the next stage. He was a doctor, he'd get it. Was she rushing him? But she had to know. 'There's more. I'm not sure what you mean when you say I can have the whole nine yards, husband and family, but if we're heading anywhere together then you'd have to be tested for the CF gene.'

Dan's smile was so tender she nearly cried.

'Sarah, trust me, I understand that.'

Did he understand she'd like him to do it sooner rather than later? That she needed to know the answer before she could make other decisions about their future together?

Because if he had the gene she'd have to walk away and forget about having his babies. That would be doing the right thing by Dan. She could do it. But leaving would be so hard. Dan and Leah had shown her she could love and, more importantly, they loved her back.

Tuesday night and their lovemaking was unhurried, and exquisitely tender. Sarah had never known that desire could uncoil so agonisingly slowly that every cell in her body was dancing as they waited for the promised release.

'Pinch me,' Sarah whispered. 'I'm not sure that wasn't a dream.'

'Oh, it was real, every last bit of it.' Dan wrapped her in his arms and kissed the top of her head.

Every muscle in her body refused to move. Her mind was a cloud of spent desire. How Dan could take her to the edge and hold her there for so long, tantalising her, making her almost beg to be released.

He said into her hair, 'Wish I hadn't agreed to go camping tomorrow.'

'How long will you be away?' Because the trip had been put off for so long she'd begun to believe he wouldn't be going away.

'Four days at the most.'

'What?' she cried. 'You do what you've just done to me and then tell me you're gone for days?' She'd miss him like crazy. 'Where is this camp site?'

A deep chuckle erupted somewhere above her head. 'You're stroking my ego something terrible. Keep going like that and I'll believe anything's possible.'

'Like what?'

Dan slid down the bed until his face was opposite hers. 'Like coming camping with us.'

'Me?' What a ridiculous idea! She had a job to do in

town. 'Do you think the others would appreciate being kept awake by your passionate cries throughout the night?'

'I can do quiet.'

'For sure.' Sarah snuggled closer. 'I am going to miss you, and not just because of the sex.'

Dan stroked her back. 'Do you think you might like to try camping some time? We could go for a night one weekend while you're still here.'

'Me? In a tent? No hot and cold water, no coffee, wearing clothes I wouldn't be seen dead in?' She poked him lightly in the ribs. 'Get real.'

'I was.'

She chuckled. 'I guess anything's possible given enough time. After all, I do wear gumboots these days.' This guy made her do and say things she'd never have believed a few weeks ago. Now caution and excitement mingled in her veins.

'I'd buy you another pair of gumboots, this time with possum fur.'

'Now you're bribing me.'

'That was only an opening bid. You gave up too easily.'

She grinned. 'What else was on offer?'

'My body.'

'Doesn't count. I can get that with one touch.' And she proceeded to show him how easily persuaded he could be.

Further into the night Sarah lay on her side, Dan spooned behind her with his arm over her waist. Despite her languorous body, she was wide awake.

Dan was out of it, so soundly asleep a ten-ton truck driving through the front door wouldn't have woken him. She was storing up all the sensations from his hand splayed across her tummy to his breaths on the back of her neck, from his hard thighs against the back of her legs to the occasional light snore.

She hugged herself. She loved Dan. What more could she ask for?

Dan's love, that's what. And for him to take that gene test. It was starting to burn at her that he hadn't said any more about it since her revelation on Saturday. It had been hard to tell him, then she'd got nothing back since. *Patience*, she warned herself. But she didn't do patience, not when she was desperate to know his take on the situation. Not when this same scenario had backfired on her with Oliver. When would Dan have the test? Would he have it at all?

She tensed. Why should he? They hadn't made a commitment to a joint future. He didn't owe her anything. She was getting way ahead of herself. Comfortable in Port Weston, in love with Dan, desperate to have children.

She rolled over and looked at his sleeping form. Way, way ahead of yourself, Sarah. This is the affair you wanted to have with him. Nothing more, nothing less. Dan may have helped you move on from Oliver, he may have shown you how to love again, but there had never been any promises beyond that. He hadn't even promised that much.

She had less than three weeks left here. Did she spend them in Dan's bed? Or alone in hers?

The sound of a vehicle in the drive woke Dan next morning. The bedside clock read six. 'Who's that at this god-awful hour?'

He rolled over. Where was Sarah? His hand groped across the other side of the bed. The sheets were cold. He sat up. 'Sarah?'

The house was silent, ominously silent. He leapt out of bed and ran, naked, to her bedroom, then the bathroom still warm from the shower having been run on hot, the kitchen where the blinds had been raised and the kettle was warm to his touch. Sarah was nowhere to be seen. Outside her car had gone.

'Strange, I didn't hear the phone.' He'd check with the hospital to see if she'd been called in for an emergency.

'Sarah's not here,' the A and E nurse informed him. 'And we haven't called for her. It's been the quietest night on record.'

Then where had she gone? Walking the beach had become a regular habit for her now but the sky was bucketing down. Not looking good for camping, though John had assured him it would be fine by midmorning. Dan banged the phone down. That cold side of his bed bothered him. Had Sarah gone back to her room after they'd made love? He shook his head. She never did that. She reckoned the after-match cuddles were almost as good as the sex. The lovemaking. Sex sounded too...too impersonal, uninvolved. No, they made love.

Love? Making love didn't mean he was in love. Did it? Gulp. He'd been thinking it might be time to find a woman to share his life with but this was for real. He wanted Sarah, in his bed, in his life, alongside him as he dealt with all life's vagaries.

But was he ready? What if Sarah wanted to return to the city? Could he go with her? Leave his family behind? He sucked air through his teeth. Could he really do that? He'd hate it, no doubt. But asking Sarah to stay here meant asking her to leave her family behind. A family who had let her down big time. But still her family. How did she feel about leaving Auckland and her dad? If she didn't want to then he was prepared to give the city a go.

He flicked the kettle on and spooned coffee granules into a mug. A new mug that matched the other new mugs and cups in the cupboard. Piece by piece Sarah was making her mark on his home. Which had only been a place to grab some sleep and feed his daughter until Sarah had come along.

Last night their lovemaking had been even more magical than ever. Sarah had seemed very happy as they'd lain talking afterwards. He'd sensed she didn't want him going away today. So wouldn't that mean she'd be here to say goodbye to him with a few hot kisses to last him until he got back? What about Leah? Surely Sarah would've wanted to give her a hug before they disappeared for a few days?

Now dressed in jeans and nothing else, Dan stood at the window, his coffee growing cold as he watched the rain pelting down on the drive and paths. Had he missed something? Had Sarah gone from the house to get away from him? So she didn't have to see him until he got back from up the valley?

He ran the previous couple of days through his mind, looking for any clues. She'd been a bit preoccupied at times, but he'd put that down to work. She'd had a busy weekend almost from the moment they'd returned from Bea's, with a couple of tricky procedures that had had her phoning specialist surgeons she knew in Auckland.

For the first time in ages Celine popped into his mind. She used to stop talking to him, go out for a day without telling him where she'd gone. His stomach began churning. All the old guilt bubbled up, threatened to overwhelm him. He'd struggled to get through to her when she'd been like that, thinking the depression had had something to do with her reaction to him. What if he was the problem? Sarah was not depressed and yet she'd left the house this morning without a word to him.

No, history could not be repeating itself. Last night Sarah had been so loving, so willing. And afterwards she'd wrapped her body around his, holding him against her like she'd never let go. What had happened, what had entered her mind in the early hours of the morning that had driven her out of his bed?

Cystic fibrosis. The gene she carried. Should he have talked more about that with her? It would be a major issue in any lasting relationship Sarah was involved in. His heart squeezed for her. How hard had it been for her to tell him? Had she told him now in case they took this affair to the next level? Giving him time to digest it, make his mind up on how he felt? Had she been let down in the past? By Oliver? Questions banged around inside his skull, and the lack of answers raised his anxiety level.

When she'd told him he'd filed it away, something to think about in the future if they continued together. There'd be tests for him to have done, decisions to make if the results showed him to be a carrier as well. But Sarah would've wanted to have some indication on how he felt immediately. It would've been hard for her to tell him. Damn it, he hadn't been very understanding. At least he could rectify his blunder, starting this morning, before he headed away.

So where was she?

Sarah pushed her plate aside and reached for the coffee George had just made. 'That was excellent. I should start every day with a cooked breakfast.'

Opposite her Jill finished the last of her scrambled eggs. 'This baby sure gives me an appetite.'

Sarah laughed. 'At how many months?'

'Who's counting?' Jill buttered a slice of toast, smothered it in marmalade. 'Seriously, I'm always hungry at the moment. If that doesn't stop soon, I'll have to start being careful. Don't want to end up looking like the Michelin Man.'

Sarah rolled her eyes. 'No chance.'

'So…' Jill eyed Sarah over her toast. 'How's things going with my brother-in-law?'

'Fine.' Sarah's muttered understatement earned her a wink. 'Truly.'

'We all know that,' Jill drawled.

'All? Who's all?' Did the whole town about their affair?

'Oh, you know, family.' Jill shrugged her shoulders, but as Sarah tried to relax, Jill added, 'And the theatre staff, Charlie, these guys.' She glanced over at George and Robert working behind the counter.

Sarah gulped. Definitely the whole town. 'Tell me you're joking.'

'Everyone cares about you two, wants to see you both happy.'

'They don't know me.'

'They know you've made Dan smile again, that Leah loves you, that you're a superb surgeon who cares about her patients enough to go in before hitting the pillow late at night so she can make them feel better.'

'Like any surgeon would do.' Patients liked reassurance, especially at night when pain kept them awake and the doubts started rolling in. But she hadn't done a lot of that back in Auckland.

Jill's phone gave a muffled ring from the depths of her handbag. 'Odd,' she muttered when she read the incoming number. 'A and E. Why are they calling me before you?'

Because my phone's not switched on in case Dan tries to call. She didn't have an explanation for not being there this morning, not one she was prepared to give him anyway. But her pager should've gone off. Tugging it off her belt, she was surprised there was no message.

'Sarah's with me. We're on our way.' Jill snapped her phone shut. 'That was Tony. You're needed in the delivery suite. Like now.'

'What's up?'

'It's Cathy. She went into labour late yesterday but apparently everything's progressing too slowly. She has a history of pre-eclampsia, and Tony's considering a Caesarean section.'

'That's why he wants me.' She'd done sections, but not recently.

'Let's go, then.'

George stepped in front of her. 'Sarah, would you like to come to dinner tomorrow night? Not in the café but upstairs in our flat. The three of us.'

She blinked. 'I'd love that.' What was that about?

'See you around seven for a drink first.'

Dan's vehicle was in the car park when they pulled up at the hospital. Guilt tugged at Sarah. Would he be angry at her? That was the last thing she wanted, and yet she couldn't blame him if he was. She'd have been hurt if he'd done the same thing to her. But she'd needed to put space between them before she blew up and said things best left alone. Things like he couldn't be trusted to do the one thing that was ultra-important to her, just like her ex hadn't. Never mind that Dan hadn't known about the gene for more than a couple of days, she felt desperate to know that he could be relied on.

But there wasn't time for him right now. Jill had said Tony sounded very worried.

Tony was waiting outside Cathy's room. 'Thanks for coming in so quickly.'

Sarah got straight to the point. 'Details?'

'Cathy's blood pressure is 170 over 120, and rising. She's got excessive fluid retention and protein in her urine.'

Sarah frowned at the abnormal results. 'And the baby?'

'Prolonged tachycardia. Heart rate of 138 beats per minute five minutes ago.'

'Doesn't sound like we've got any choice but to retrieve the baby.' A racing foetal heart rate was serious.

Tony looked behind Sarah. 'Hi, Dan. Have you come in to help with this one?'

Sarah's heart thumped as she turned. 'Morning, Dan.' He looked wary, not angry.

'I'm available if Sarah needs me. I'm not going up the valley until after lunch.' Dan's eyes didn't leave Sarah's face and she could feel her cheeks heating up. 'I missed you this morning. You left very early.'

'I was restless and you were sleeping soundly.' Disbelief gleamed back at her. 'Jill and I went for breakfast at the café.'

'I tried phoning you to say have a good week, but I kept getting voice mail.'

Her tongue licked her dry lips. 'Sorry, I forgot to turn it on.' The lie was rancid in her mouth. 'Did you come to see Cathy?'

'Brent called me so I decided to drop by, offer him some support,' Dan said.

There was a huge question in his eyes, making her feel mean. She turned away, following the GP in to see Cathy. 'Hi, Cathy. Tony has filled me in on your details. He's called me in for your Caesarean.'

Cathy's eyes widened. 'Sarah, thank you for coming in. I'm really pleased you're doing the operation. Hey, hello, Dan.'

'Hey, how's my favourite cousin?' Dan leaned down to kiss her cheek before turning to a very worried-looking Brent and squeezing his shoulder.

'Not so flash right now.' Cathy had indentations in her bottom lip from pressing her teeth down, presumably during contractions. Her face was grey, another indication that things were not right. She looked to Sarah, a plea in her eyes. 'Is my baby going to be all right?'

Sarah winced inwardly. As yet she didn't know all the details so she wasn't about to make a promise she mightn't be able to keep. But she understood Cathy's fear. 'I certainly intend doing all I can to help ensure that it is.' Then she turned to Brent. 'How are you coping?'

'I'm feeling as useless as snow-boots in the desert. If only I could do something for Cathy.' His voice rose, and his Adam's apple bobbed in his throat.

Poor guy. 'It seems harder for the fathers in these situations.'

Cathy's eyes squeezed tight and her hands clenched Brent's. Her knuckles were white as pain racked her body. Beads of sweat popped out across her brow and the midwife sponged her face. Her breast rose and fell rapidly as she struggled to breathe. 'Pain. It's…not…the…contraction.'

'Take your time, breathe through the contraction,' the midwife instructed.

'Not a contraction.' Cathy struggled to speak. 'In my chest. Pain in my chest. I can't get air.'

The midwife glanced at the GP, then Sarah, one eyebrow slightly raised, before she slipped an oxygen mask over her patient's mouth and nose. Cathy's breathing deepened, not back to normal but better than it had been before the intervention of the oxygen supply.

Sarah finished perusing the notes Tony had handed her. 'Let's go. I'll page Hamish now.'

'He's here somewhere. His car's outside,' Dan informed her. Then he leaned close and whispered, 'Do you want me to assist you?'

A wee sigh of relief slid through her lips. Despite everything, having Dan there made operating so much easier. 'Definitely. That chest pain makes me wonder if something else's going on here.'

'I agree, but we'll take it one step at a time.'

Sarah wanted to touch Dan, hug him, but that would be giving him the wrong message after that morning. It was confusing her. How could she stay away from him during her last weeks here? 'Let's go scrub up.'

Everything happened in a rush. Hamish arrived almost before Sarah had finished paging him, and went straight to see Cathy.

Sarah told Dan, 'Antenatal patients are not my forte. They go to the obstetricians and gynaecologists, not to our clinic.'

Dan nodded. 'I guess I do have the upper hand in this case.'

'I'm quite okay about you taking the lead.' She wasn't about to stand on her high horse about his leave when two patients relied on her.

'How about I talk you through the procedure? Then if another case comes your way over the next few weeks, you'll have this one behind you.'

It wasn't likely to happen but Sarah acquiesced. 'Good idea. Let's get moving. Cathy can't afford to wait longer than necessary.'

Standing beside the operating table, Sarah picked up the scalpel and asked everyone, 'Are we ready?' Then she was pushing down into the swollen flesh that protected a little life.

Michael Ross was born with the umbilical cord wound around his neck. Sarah held him while Dan expertly removed the cord. Their reward was a shrieking, ear-piercing squall. A woozy Cathy watched him hungrily through tear-filled eyes. 'He's beautiful.'

By the time Sarah finished repairing the incision she'd made to retrieve the baby Cathy was alert and eager to hold the precious bundle a nurse had wrapped in a tiny cotton blanket. Thankfully nothing had gone wrong and her earlier concerns had disappeared. Sarah watched as the mother held her son for the very first time.

Cathy had eyes only for her son. The world could've imploded right then and she wouldn't have noticed. She certainly wasn't aware of the orderly wheeling her out into Recovery, where Brent waited anxiously.

Sarah followed, and told Brent, 'I don't think I need to say anything. Your wife and son are doing well.'

'He's a noisy little blighter,' Brent said around a face-splitting grin. He leaned over and kissed Cathy on her cheek, then carefully took his son's tiny fist in his.

Sarah watched them, enthralled. Along with Cushla, they made a perfect family. They'd be busy but she didn't doubt they'd cope.

'You okay?' Dan touched her arm lightly.

'Yes. Isn't this the most beautiful sight?' She nodded at Cathy holding her baby. What did it feel like to hold your baby that first time?

Dan nodded. 'It is. I still remember Leah's birth. The moment I saw her, holding her tiny body, so afraid I'd break her, the instant love that overwhelmed me. It's magic.'

The wonder in his voice made Sarah's eyes fill. She'd love to have Dan's child. She'd love to give him that magic moment again. Would he have that test done? Did it matter if he didn't? Ah, hello. Where had *that* weird idea come from?

'We'll call in later,' Dan told the happy couple.

'Thanks.' Both parents barely lifted their heads from their son to acknowledge him.

Dan took Sarah's elbow and led her out of the room.

'I'm heading home to pick up the tent and other things.' He paused. 'Is there anything you need, Sarah?' His thumb traced a line down her cheek, along her jaw. His eyes were dark with confusion.

Yes, a test result. A hug. Some understanding of why I'm so impatient and tense. 'Not at the moment.'

'I guess I'll get going, then.' He stood in front of her, searching her face. Looking for what? An answer to her behaviour?

'Have a good time. Don't let the sand flies bite too often.' She started to lean in to kiss him, thought better of it, and backed away. If she was going to cut the ties then now was the time to start.

Dan watched her stride away. Her shoulders were tugged tight, her back ramrod straight, her steps a little longer and louder than usual. He was definitely on the outer and none the wiser about why. Deep inside a dull ache began to throb. With it came memories of trying to understand Celine, trying to help her when she hadn't wanted to be helped. Was this the same scenario?

Had Sarah come to a decision about returning to Auckland at the end of the month? If she had, could he blame her? He hadn't given her any indications about his feelings. Because he was only beginning to understand them himself. And needed to know exactly how he felt before he made a move.

Jill appeared at his elbow. 'You okay?'

'Yes, of course.' Dan turned to his sister-in-law, saw the concern radiating from her eyes. 'Actually, I haven't got a clue.'

'She needs you as much as you need her. Don't let the past get in the way.' Jill stood on tiptoe and kissed his chin.

And then she was gone, heading for Theatre and the next patient.

'Easy to say,' Dan murmured. But he had a plan. Sarah had been hurt in the past, and so had he. One of them had to make the first move, break the mould that held them both tied to their pasts. So he went to find Tony.

CHAPTER ELEVEN

'SINCE it's such a beautiful evening, we'll sit out on the deck, if that's all right with you.' George told Sarah when she arrived the next night, a huge bunch of summer flowers in her hand.

'Perfect.' Sarah sighed. 'This is heaven.' Well, it would be if Dan were here to share it with her.

'Isn't it? We took a long while to settle here after the pace of Christchurch, but now we'd never leave. This is a little piece of paradise and the locals are delightful.' Robert sat in the chair beside Sarah. 'Port Weston grows on you, if you let it.'

Looking out over the rooftops of the main street shops to the ocean beyond, Sarah was startled to realise she agreed. 'Auckland seems so far away.'

'It is.'

Throughout the meal Sarah found her mind wandering back to that thought. Odd, but she hadn't missed anything or anyone from home. Not the social events, not the restaurants, the shops, or the clinic. She had been born and bred in the city, so when had she shed that persona? Or was it lurking, ready to take up again the moment she pointed the Jag northward?

Robert placed coffee and Cointreau in front of her. 'Port Weston's got under your skin. Already.'

Not Port Weston, but the people living there. Especially one man. Sipping the liqueur, she savoured the heavy orange tang on her tongue, and asked, 'So what do I do now?'

'Stay. It's as simple as that.'

'And as complex.' She couldn't stay if Dan didn't want her.

George leaned across the table and touched the back of her hand. 'Only you make it complicated. It's hard, shedding all those commitments you have in your other life, but if you want to, you'll find a way.'

'Thanks a bundle.' She knew he was right but this feeling of having found her place could be false. It could evaporate as quickly as it had taken her over. And if Dan didn't want her here then she couldn't encroach on his territory.

'We know what we're talking about,' Robert added.

The three of them sat in comfortable silence for a few minutes. Then George drew a deep breath. 'Sarah, we invited you here for a reason. Not that we didn't want to have a meal with you, of course.'

George spoke so quietly Sarah looked at him out of the corner of her eye. He was watching Robert with such tenderness she felt her heart squeeze. They were very lucky to have found each other.

Quietly, in a flat voice, Robert told her, 'George wants me to have my leg operated on. The pain's getting progressively worse and I don't sleep much at nights. I try not to disturb him but I know I do.'

Her heart blocked her throat. Was this what she thought it was? She said nothing, just waited.

'I'm having the operation done.' A quiver rattled his voice and the eyes he raised to her were heavy with fear. 'And I want you to do it.'

'Thank you for your trust in me.' Wow, Dan had said she could get Robert to change his mind, and it seemed she had without saying a single word. She asked softly, 'What went wrong last time?'

'I nearly died. Twice. My heart stopped while I was on the operating table. Then my leg got infected and they couldn't control it.' He reached for her hand, gripped it hard. 'It was terrifying.'

'You're not going to die.' Sarah squeezed his hand in return.

'I hope not.' The smile he gave her was twisted and sad and filled with fear.

'Robert, I'll need your authority to talk to your previous surgeon and to get your files.'

Sarah shivered. Was she up to this? The surgery didn't faze her, but helping these two men worried her. They'd become friends. She closed her eyes and hoped Dan's belief in her was realistic. Then she had an idea.

'George, Robert, of course I'll do the operation unless I find it is beyond me. But how would you feel about Dan assisting me?' She held her breath, not knowing why they'd come to her, a relative newcomer, and not gone to Dan, whom they were very close to.

The men looked at each and nodded. 'We'd be very happy,' George told her. 'You two are a team in everything you do. I'd have been surprised if you hadn't wanted Dan there.'

Some of the tension that had begun tightening her muscles slipped away. She might have personal issues to sort out with Dan but she needed him by her side when she performed this operation. Robert had become a friend and his fear made her nervous.

'Right,' she said. 'Let's talk.' And she spoke quietly, knowledgably, drawing on all her experience with distressed patients.

* * *

Sarah tentatively scheduled Robert's surgery for the evening two days away, worried to leave it any longer in case he changed his mind. Every spare minute of the next day was spent talking to specialists, calling in Robert's medical records to study and discussing with his previous cardiologist what had happened during the first operation. Hamish agreed to be the anaesthetist and she kept him appraised of everything.

She dropped into the café at lunchtime to reassure Robert. Over a double shot, long black, George tried to voice his gratitude for Sarah getting his partner this far already.

'It's unbelievable. I've been hoping and praying he'd have this done for so long now, and here…' He stopped, unable to finish his sentence.

Sarah leaned forward and touched his hand. 'It's not me you have to thank, it's Robert. He's a very brave man.'

It was nearly six that night when she tossed her theatre scrubs into the laundry basket and changed into jeans and a T-shirt. Outside she waved the key at the Jag to unlock it and slid behind the steering-wheel. A dull ache throbbed behind her eyes as she smoothed out the rough map Jill had drawn for her.

Finding the camping site was unbelievably easy, even for a city girl. Six tents were clustered along the flat grassed area above the river. A fire flickered within a circle of rocks. When Sarah pushed her door open, the harsh pitch of crickets filled the air.

'Sarah?' Dan approached the car. 'What brings you out here? Is something wrong?'

Darn, but he looked so good. Big and strong, his hair a riot of curls, his shorts revealing those muscular thighs she loved to run her hands down. How could she even think about heading north? Leaving Dan?

'Sarah?' Fingers caught her shoulders and his large hands shook her gently. 'What brings you up the valley?'

She swallowed. 'Firstly, there's nothing wrong.' She felt him relax. 'I need to ask something of you. It's important.' She looked up into those eyes that missed nothing, and silently begged him not to walk away as she deserved.

'Sure. Just let me tell the others we're taking a walk.' Was that hope lacing his words? Did he think she'd come to explain why she'd left his bed during the night last time they made love?

'Sarah, Sarah!' Leah exploded out of a tent, making a beeline for her.

Sarah's heart rolled over as she bent to catch the human speedball. 'Hey, gorgeous. How's my favourite girl?'

'Have you come to stay in our tent? Daddy takes up all the space. I have to curl up tight.' Leah's nose pressed into Sarah's neck, and Sarah inhaled her scent.

'It's so good to see you, sweetheart. I've come to talk to Daddy.' Then Sarah looked up and saw a shadow cross Dan's eyes. Had she made a mistake? Would he prefer she didn't act so affectionately with his daughter if she was leaving town? How could she not?

Within moments Sarah was surrounded by Bea, John and everyone else. It took a few minutes before Dan could persuade Leah to stay with Bea while he and Sarah went down to the river for a walk.

They sat on a large flat rock, their legs dangling over the water. Sarah batted away a mosquito and looked across at Dan. 'Robert's asked me to operate on his leg.'

'I knew you'd persuade him.' Disappointment and admiration mingled in Dan's eyes, making her feel sad and proud at the same time. She hoped he didn't feel peeved he hadn't been the one Robert had asked.

'No, you're wrong. He came to me.' She held his gaze. 'Dan, I need your help with this. Will you assist me? Tomorrow night.'

He looked away, looked back. 'Of course. But why? It's not difficult surgery.'

Everything her life had come to mean in Port Weston— friendship, love, belonging—was tied up in this particular operation. And, unusually, she feared failure. Sarah laid her hand on Dan's. 'Not difficult and yet the hardest I've had to do because he's a real friend. That's what this place has done to me. I know I'll be fine if you're there with me.'

His eyes sharpened, his hand under hers tensed. But he only said, 'I'll come back with you now. Leah will be happy staying with Bea. They're back the day after tomorrow.' He stood and looked down at her. 'We'll split tomorrow's theatre list so that you're not exhausted for Robert's surgery.'

He understood. He was coming to help her. And yet she knew she'd let him down. Had he been hoping for more? She wanted to explain her actions but couldn't without sounding like she was begging him for a place in his life. A place with conditions.

Because Dan had taken over half the surgical list Robert's surgery was brought forward to early afternoon. There were no problems, only one nasty surprise. When Sarah opened up the leg, she exclaimed in horror. The offending tendon had somehow got twisted before being rejoined.

'Working with you is a treat,' Sarah told Dan as they finished up. 'We seem to understand each other instinctively.'

'Not only in Theatre.' His eyes glowered back at her over his mask.

'I know.' But at the moment there were things they had to sort through to understand each fully.

In Recovery she told a groggy Robert, 'Your foot will take some work so you can walk without a limp, but at least the pain will be gone.'

Robert smiled the blank smile of a patient coming out of anaesthesia and promptly vomited into the stainless-steel bowl Jill held below his face.

'That's gratitude for you.' Sarah patted Robert's shoulder. 'I'll see you later.'

Outside in the waiting room she found Dan reassuring George that the operation had been a success and that there'd been none of the complications of last time.

There were tears in George's eyes when he gripped Sarah's hand to thank her. 'You don't know what this means to both of us.'

'Yes, I do. Great coffee, and lots of it,' she quipped, before giving him a hard hug. It was unbelievably good to have done something for people she had come to care about.

'I've got to go and pick Leah up from Bea's. It's been raining up the valley all day so they packed up camp,' Dan said.

'Give her a hug from me.'

'You can give her one yourself tonight. Unless you've now found somewhere else to stay?'

'Not at all. I'll see you later, then.' Sarah watched him go, her heart breaking. They were well matched, if only she could believe he wanted more than an affair.

'Sarah, we've got a man coming in from the mine.

Something about a head injury,' Hamish called from the door.

'On my way.' At least she wouldn't have time to think about Dan for a while.

Dan stopped in the doorway. His heart blocked his throat. Yearning stabbed him.

Sarah sat on the edge of Cathy's bed, baby Michael in her arms, a look of wonder on her face. Deep longing was in her eyes, in the careful way she held the precious bundle, in her total absorption with the wee boy.

Dan's feet were stuck to the floor. This was what he wanted too. With Sarah. He'd told her once she'd be a great mum, and he believed it even more now.

'I want to hold Michael.' Leah's voice cut across the room, jerking Dan's attention away from this beautiful woman to find Jill and Cathy watching him with smiles on their faces.

Sarah's head came up, her eyes seeking his. 'Hi,' she whispered.

'Hi,' Dan replied softly, love winding through his gut.

Jill sat Leah beside Sarah and took the baby, helping Leah hold the enfant. They all watched Leah, saw her face light up as she peered down at Michael. Then she looked up at Dan and Dan stared back. He knew what was coming, could see it in her innocent eyes. And, like standing in the path of an oncoming avalanche, there was nothing he could do to stop it.

'Daddy, why can't we have a baby?'

Dan stepped forward, not sure what to do, what to say. 'Leah, we just can't, okay?' And he glanced at Sarah.

Her face had paled. Her hands were fists in her lap.

'Why?' Leah persisted. 'I want one.'

Sarah turned to Leah. 'You've got to have a mother to have a baby.'

Leah's eyes widened. 'Why?'

'So the baby can grow in her tummy.' Sarah grimaced.

Leah gazed at Sarah, adoration in her eyes. 'You can be the mummy. Please, Sarah, please.'

'Leah,' Dan cut across the suddenly still room. 'That's enough.'

Sarah leapt up, her face drained of all colour, her eyes wild. She shoved past Dan in the doorway and was gone, tearing down the hall.

Dan snapped at Jill, 'Watch out for Leah,' and he was racing out after Sarah.

An ache grew in Sarah's chest. Mummy. That's the only word she could hear, bouncing around in her head. Bing-bong. Mummy. Mummy.

'Sarah, wait.' Dan's deep voice boomed out behind her.

She didn't slow down at all. Hauled the outside door open, charged out into the rose gardens.

Then Dan was running beside her, matching her step for step. His hand folded around hers, but he didn't try to stop her. Instead they kept running until they reached the car park on the other side.

'Sarah,' he gasped, and then he spun around in front of her and gripped her shoulders, absorbing the force of her forward momentum as she ran into him. His arms encircled her and he held her tight, his chin on her head, his fast breaths stirring her hair.

She tried to pull away. He tightened his hold.

'Let me go.'

'Only if you agree to come with me.'

What? Where? 'Why would I go with you? If you're gong to give me a hard time for getting Leah's hopes up then do it now, get it over with.'

'Sarah.' He leaned back at the waist to look down at her. 'I want to show you something.'

'Why?' She didn't understand. What did that have to do with what Leah had just said?

His finger lifted her chin so she had to look him in the eye. 'Will you trust me on this?'

Totally perplexed, she could only nod.

Within moments they were in the Land Cruiser, tearing down the drive and out onto the main road. She sat frozen while a million questions whirled around her brain. And then the vehicle slowed, turned in through a gate, the wheels bouncing over the rough terrain.

She jerked around to stare at Dan. His finger settled over her lips. 'Shh. Save all those questions. I asked you to trust me, remember?'

She nodded slowly. What the hell was going on?

Then he was delving into the back of the vehicle, bringing her gumboots to her door. 'Put these on.' He swapped his shoes for boots. He took her hand and began leading her across the ankle-deep, wet grass.

'Here.' Dan pulled her to a stop, turned her around and dropped his arm over her shoulders. 'Look at that view. Isn't it spectacular?'

The air was misty, and behind them the sea pounded the shore. Her breath caught in her throat. 'Simply beautiful.' But?

'Imagine a house built right here, a long house with this view from every room.'

Her heart began a steady thumping. 'A house?'

'Our house, Sarah. With lots of bedrooms for all those children we want. And a huge vegetable garden over there by that old pump shed. We'd have paddocks for horses, plenty of room for a dog to run around.' His hand tightened on her shoulder, pulling her closer to him. 'What do you say?'

The thumping got louder. Her tongue slid across her bottom lip. The picture he'd just painted was so real she could taste it in the air, see it in every direction she looked. It was everything she wanted with the man she loved. She wanted to say, shout, *What about those children?* What about the CF? But he'd asked her to trust him. And she knew deep down he'd never hurt her, never abuse that trust. And if she couldn't return that trust then she shouldn't be here.

She turned, slid her arms around his neck. 'I say yes. Yes, to all of it.'

Those blue eyes lightened, that wide mouth stretched into the most beautiful smile she'd ever seen. 'I love you, Sarah, with all my heart, and then some.'

'I love you, too. You sneaked in under my skin when I wasn't looking.' She stretched up on her toes, reaching her mouth to his.

Then he stopped her short. 'I had a sample taken and sent away to be tested for the cystic fibrosis gene the other day. The result will take a while to come through.'

Her heart slowed. She'd been right to trust him. He'd never let her down, never hide from his children's needs. 'Thank you,' she whispered against his mouth before her lips claimed his.

A kiss filled with promise. Not matter what the future brought them, their love would get them through.

EPILOGUE

SARAH stopped what she was doing to stare out across the lawn of their new home down to the pounding surf on the beach beyond. Those resolutions and new beginnings she had thought impossible almost a year ago had multiplied tenfold, making her happy beyond her wildest dreams. Today would tie everything, everyone, together perfectly.

A light kick on her hand made her smile, and she looked down at the most precious gift of all. 'Hello, gorgeous.' She bent over to kiss the fat tummy in front of her.

Davey gurgled back at her and kicked her chin.

'Thanks, buster.' Now for the job that had others in the house running for the beach. Holding her beautiful, healthy son's feet, she lifted his bottom and wiped it clean.

'Ooh, poo. That's gross.' Leah danced beside her. 'Boys are disgusting.'

Dan laughed from the safety of the doorway. 'We are not.'

'Not you, Daddy. You're not a boy, you're old.'

'Thanks a lot, missy.'

'Not as old as Santa.' Leah bounced all the way across the lounge to the huge pine tree in the corner, looking sweet in her lovely gold dress. She bent over, hands on hips, inspecting the bounty underneath.

Decorated in white and gold bows, glittering balls and

curling ribbons, their Christmas tree was perfect. Many presents lay around the base, constantly being shifted and sorted by a certain impatient young madam.

At a second change table Jill snapped plastic pants in place over baby Amy's clean nappy. 'Give Leah a few years and Dan will be wishing she still thought boys were gross.'

'I'm sure you're right.' Dan ventured close enough to drop a kiss on Sarah's brow and tickle his son's tummy. 'Can I get you two ladies a drink? One for the nerves, so to speak.'

'Oh, right, now he comes near. Brave man.' Sarah grinned as she handed him the bucket containing the offensive nappy. 'And by the way, my nerves are rock steady.' But her heart ran a little faster than normal, and she hadn't been able to eat breakfast. 'I'd love some wine but guess it will have to be OJ.' Breastfeeding had put a halt to some pleasures but had given her a whole heap of new ones. Four weeks old and growing by the minute, Davey had a voracious appetite for someone so small.

Dan didn't carry the gene but, while relieved, Sarah had discovered she'd have been more than able to cope if the test result had gone the other way. With Dan, anything was possible.

Jill lifted Amy into her arms and came to stand by Sarah. 'It's going to be a long time before I'll be touching anything remotely alcoholic.'

'I thought you were giving up feeding—' Sarah saw the glow in Jill's eyes. 'Oh, Jill. You're not? When?' She hugged her closest friend, careful not to squash Amy between them.

'September again.'

'You don't waste any time, do you? What wonderful news.' Sarah turned to dress Davey in a clean nappy, then tugged on his black pants and a white shirt to match his father's.

She glanced around, looking for Dan, expecting to see him caught up talking to a guest. But, no, there he was, walking towards her, two long-stem glasses held between the fingers of one hand. Her heart rolled over, her tummy did its melting thing. Dressed in new, fitted black trousers and a crisp white shirt, he looked absolutely wonderful. Mouth-watering. Sarah pinched herself, still struggling to believe how lucky she was that she'd found this man, the one man in the world guaranteed to make her weak at the knees. And even better, a man who loved her as deeply as she loved him.

He winked at her, a long, slow wink designed to make her helpless with desire.

'You shouldn't have done that.' She smiled back the kind of sweet, wide, tip-of-teeth-showing smile that got to him every time.

Dan laughed, loud and, oh, so carefree. 'Touché.'

Jill spun around to gawp at him. 'I still can't get used to you being so relaxed that you laugh at everything.'

Picking Davey up, Sarah glanced outside again. The lawn was filling up with people. The marquee to the side also contained its share of visitors. 'Who didn't Dan invite?'

'Old Joey.' Dan answered her rhetorical question from beside her. 'Actually, I did invite him but he had to catch a trout for Christmas dinner tomorrow. That's his way of saying he doesn't like to socialise.'

'That's sad.'

Dan raised those imperious eyebrows at her. '*You* think?'

She chuckled. 'Yes, I know. I remember that night I

came home to find a party in full swing. I wanted to head out of town.'

When she'd arrived in Port Weston she'd known no one and now look at all these people. She saw Pat, Malcolm, George and Robert. Bea and John. Family, friends, the new surgeon and his young wife who'd moved into the hospital house last week in preparation to working alongside Dan and her. Never in her wildest dreams, when she'd muttered 'new beginnings' that first day parked on the cliff top, had she envisaged being part of something so wonderful, of belonging to such an extensive and caring family.

And even more surprising were those two people sitting on the couch—at opposite ends—listening earnestly to Leah's explanation about how Santa would be squeezing down the chimney that night. Sarah gently nudged her son's cheek with her nose. 'Let's go and talk to Grandpa and Grandma.'

'Here you go, Dad. Your grandson wants time with you.' She handed her father the baby, and stood with her heart in her throat, watching the awe grow in her father's eyes. Her mother shuffled along the couch to be close to Davey. Or was it to be close to Dad?

They'd come separately, but were staying in the same motel in town. George had informed Sarah her parents had been for brunch at the café—together. And that they'd talked for ages. Good, happy talk, not acrimonious stuff. George's words. Sarah could only hope her parents might find their way back to each other.

Her father looked up at her, clearing his throat. 'I did my best for you at the time.'

'I know that now, Dad.' It had taken years, and Dan, for her to learn that.

He swallowed. 'But it wasn't good enough. I'm sorry.'

No, it hadn't been, but that was all behind them. Sarah

knelt down and hugged her father and son to her. 'I wouldn't change a thing, Dad. I really wouldn't.' Otherwise she mightn't have met Dan.

A warm hand on her shoulder. Dan's breath was warm on her cheek as he leaned down to kiss her. 'Have I told you today how much I love you?'

'Hmm, let me see. Once in the shower, again after breakfast.' She stood and slid her arms around his waist. 'And definitely when you were trying to get out of changing a particularly stinky nappy.'

Dan kissed her ear lobe. 'Are we ready?'

'I've always been ready.' It had just taken a while to realise that.

'Then let's do it, Dr Livingston.'

Sarah stepped back and smoothed her ankle-length white silk dress where it touched her hips. She straightened the gold sash around her waist and leaned down to do up the straps of her pretty, thin-heeled gold sandals.

'Leah, sweetheart.' Sarah held a hand out to her daughter. 'It's time.'

Dan lifted Davey onto one arm, and took Sarah's other hand in his. He led his family outside and down the lawn. They stepped over the scattered rose petals, heading to the marriage celebrant waiting for them. On either side family and friends cheered and clapped and blew them kisses.

Tears blurred Sarah's vision and she stumbled.

Dan tightened his grip, held her from falling. 'Silly sandals. What's wrong with a pair of gumboots?'

* * * * *

Special Offers

Every month we put together collections and longer reads written by your favourite authors.

Here are some of next month's highlights— and don't miss our fabulous discount online!

On sale 16th December

On sale 16th December

On sale 6th January

Save 20% on all Special Releases